The Year of the Baby

* AN ANNA WANG NOVEL *

Read more about Anna and Laura and Camille
in the first book, *The Year of the Book*.

A JUNIOR LIBRARY GUILD SELECTION

"A feast to be devoured in one sitting . . . a pleasure to read
and more. This is a novel to treasure and share with every
middle-grade reader you know."
—*New York Times Book Review* (Editors' Choice)

"Readers are led to discover the extraordinary within the ordi-
nary, and to witness how kindness can draw trust and create
confidence in a hesitant child."
—*School Library Journal*

"A remarkably pithy and nuanced portrait of a fourth-grader
and her world."
—*The Bulletin*

The Year of the Baby

* AN ANNA WANG NOVEL *

by Andrea Cheng

illustrated by Patrice Barton

Houghton Mifflin Harcourt

Boston New York

For information about permission to reproduce selections from this book, write to
Permissions, Houghton Mifflin Harcourt Publishing Company,
215 Park Avenue South, New York, New York 10003.

www.hmhco.com

The text of this book is set in Berkeley Oldstyle.
The illustrations are drawn with pen-and-ink and digitally colored.

The Library of Congress has cataloged the hardcover edition as follows:
Cheng, Andrea.
The year of the baby / by Andrea Cheng ; illustrated by Patrice Barton.
p. cm.
Sequel to: Year of the book.
Summary: Fifth-grader Anna is concerned that her baby sister Kaylee,
adopted from China three months ago, is not thriving so she and her
best friends, Laura and Camille, create a science project that may save the day.
1. Chinese Americans—Juvenile fiction. [1. Chinese Americans—Fiction. 2.
Babies—Fiction. 3. Science projects—Fiction. 4. Intercountry
adoption—Fiction. 5. Adoption—Fiction. 6. Best friends—Fiction.
7. Friendship—Fiction. 8. Schools—Fiction.]
I. Barton, Patrice, 1955– ill. II.
Title.
PZ7.C41943Yd 2013
[Fic]—dc23
2012018679

ISBN 978-0-547-91067-3 hardcover
ISBN 978-0-544-22525-1 paperback

Manufactured in the United States of America
DOC 10 9 8 7 6 5 4 3 2
4500474484

Laura   Anna   Kaylee   Camille

PRONUNCIATION GUIDE

One - Yi *(ee)* 一

Two - Er *(are)* 二

Three - *San (sun)* 三

Four - *Si (she)* 四

Five - *Wu (woo)* 五

Fifty - *Wu shi (woo she)* 五十

Goodbye - *Zai jian (tsai jian)* 再见

See you tomorrow! - *Ming tian jian (ming tian jian)* 明天见

Cat - *Mao (maow)* 猫

Grandma (mom's mom) - *Wai Po (why po)* 外婆

Girl - *Nv hai (new high)* 女孩

Hello / How are you? - *Ni hao (nee how)* 你好

Little sister - *Xiao mei mei (sheow may may)* 小妹妹

Stuffed bun - *Bao zi (bao dze)* 包子

King, *also a common last name* - *Wang (wong)* 王

Baby, *also* treasure - *Bao Bao (bow bow)* 宝宝

Fruit - *Shui guo (shway hwo)* 水果

Really good - *Zhen hao (jun how)* 真好

Very good - *Hen how (hun how)* 很好

Eat - *Chi (che)* 吃

Happy New Year - *Xin nian kuai le (shin nien kwai le)*

新年快乐

CONTENTS

One
Collecting Buckeyes

Teacher Zhen lets us out of Chinese class a few minutes early, and Camille and I head over to the buckeye tree to wait for Laura. I feel a big bump under my foot and bend down to pick up an unopened buckeye shell. Inside are three perfect buckeyes.

"I never saw a triple before," Camille says, smiling so wide that her gums show.

"One for you, one for me, and one for Laura," I say, watching Laura kick up the dry leaves as she heads toward us.

I didn't think Laura would really sign up for Chinese school. She's the only one in the whole school who's not at least half

Chinese. Plus, most of the kids in level one are only six or seven, and Laura's about to turn eleven. But she doesn't seem to mind. After class she always tells me and Camille what she learned.

"*Yi, er, san,*" Laura says, counting the buckeyes in the shell. "Hey, Anna, how do you say 'buckeye' in Chinese?"

I look at Camille since she knows more words than I do. She shakes her head. "I don't know if they even have buckeyes in China."

Laura finds two more buckeyes. "*Si, wu,*" she says, counting to five. Her words sound funny, but we can still tell what she means.

We start counting all the buckeyes. Laura takes off her sweatshirt and ties the sleeves on the bottom so we can use them like bags. When we get past *wu shi,* fifty, we lose count.

"What should we do with them?" Camille asks.

"Too bad they're not edible," Laura says. "Unless you're a squirrel."

"We could plant them," I suggest.

"Then someday we'll have a whole forest of buckeye trees," Laura says.

"And our kids can collect thousands of buckeyes," I say.

"Because they'll be best friends just like us!" Laura scoops up a handful of dry buckeye leaves and throws them above our heads.

❊ ❊ ❊

Mom pulls slowly up to the curb, gets out of the car, and heads toward Camille's mom. All the other moms are talking and laughing. My brother, Ken, and his friends are burying themselves in the leaves.

Laura's dad turns in to the school parking lot and honks. "I'd better go," she says.

"Are you at your dad's all day?" I ask. It's hard to keep track of Laura's schedule.

"Yup." She picks up her sweatshirt. It's so heavy with all the buckeyes that the sleeves drag on the ground. "*Zai jian.*" She tries hard to get the tones right.

"*Zai jian.*" Camille waves.

I hand Laura a bright red maple leaf. "*Ming tian jian.*"

"What's that mean?" she asks.

"See you tomorrow."

"*Ming tian jian,*" Laura repeats, dragging her sweatshirt with the buckeyes into the car.

Ken goes home with his friend Alan. I ask Camille if she can come over, but she has math tutoring after lunch. When we get into the car, Mom asks me if I want to help take Kaylee, my baby sister, to the doctor.

"Again?" It seems as if Kaylee has to go to the doctor every other day.

Mom starts the car. "The doctor said that it's important to monitor her closely."

Mom looks both ways twice before pulling out of the parking space. She has only had her license for about half a year, so she's still more careful than other drivers.

"Kaylee hates going to that office," I say, remembering how she clung to me as soon as we opened the door.

"Most babies are fussy at the doctor's." Mom looks in the rearview mirror and changes lanes. "She does better when you're there."

I don't really feel like going to the doctor's office, but I know Mom's right. If I don't go, Kaylee will scream the whole time. Last time I sang to her for so long that I got hoarse. It was the only thing that calmed her down.

In September when Kaylee first came from China, I thought she was perfect. I loved her little nose, her dark eyes, her big cheeks. She followed our cat, Maow Maow, from the kitchen to the living room through the dining room and back to the kitchen again. Laura, Camille, and I played with her all day except for when she fell asleep on the rug by the sofa. Then we sat around her hoping she'd hurry up and open her eyes.

The next day, Mom and I had to take her to the doctor to get her shots. First they gave her the MMR so she won't get measles, mumps, or rubella. The second shot was for meningitis, and the third one was some kind of booster. No wonder she was screaming. Then the doctor measured Kaylee's head size, her length, and her weight. She didn't say there was a problem. But when we took Kaylee back for her October checkup, her weight was exactly the same. That's when the doctor got concerned.

Mom pulls into our driveway. "If Kaylee gains this week, maybe we won't have to go back so often." The lines between her eyebrows are deep. "All we can do is keep trying."

Two

Girls Are Better

Kaylee is sitting in her highchair, banging on the tray, while Dad is trying to get her food ready. As soon as she sees me she holds out her arms.

"It's lunchtime," I say, patting her head. "We can play later."

"How was Chinese?" Dad asks.

"Fine." I can tell he's not listening, because Dad can't do more than one thing at a time and he's busy cutting a hamburger into small pieces.

I take my seat by the window. Before Mom and Dad left for China to get Kaylee, Camille's mom gave us a baby shower. We got a highchair and a car seat and sippy cups.

Everything is pink because people know that when you go to China to adopt a baby, it's a girl. Ken said he wanted a baby brother instead, but Mom said there are not many baby boys to adopt in China, unless they have health problems. When I asked why, Mom said that in China, some people favor boys.

Kaylee is starting to fuss. Dad gives her a piece of bread. She plays with it but she doesn't take a bite.

"Rice is better," Mom says, picking up the bowl of rice that Dad heated up. She puts the spoon close to Kaylee's mouth.

Kaylee opens her mouth like a baby bird. She chews for a minute, then makes a funny face and spits out the rice. It dribbles down her chin.

"Maybe she's not hungry now," I say.

"She's not used to our food yet," Mom says.

"Don't they eat a lot of rice in China?"

"Rice here and rice there is not the same," Mom says. "When I first came from China, I didn't like this rice either." Mom wipes Kaylee's mouth with a washcloth.

"How long did it take until you got used to it?"

Mom tries to remember. "Two or three years, I think."

"We can't wait that long," I say. "Maybe we can get some Chinese rice at the Asian food store."

Kaylee takes her hand that has rice stuck to it and rubs her head so there is rice mashed in her hair. I put a slice of apple on her tray. She picks it up and turns it this way and that.

"Mmmm, good," I say, taking a slice myself and putting it into my mouth.

"Mmmm," Kaylee says. She sucks on the apple for a minute.

"Do you want a hamburger?" Mom asks.

Mom makes the best hamburgers in the world, with lots of Chinese spices in them. She calls them Chinese burgers. I put one on a piece of bread, add ketchup, and cover it with another slice of bread. "Look," I say to Kaylee, taking a big bite.

Kaylee watches.

"Eat your Chinese burger," I say, pointing to the meat on her tray.

She picks up one of the pieces Dad cut for her, stares at it, and then tosses it onto the floor.

Mom looks at Dad. "A baby cannot gain weight without eating," she says.

"Give it time," Dad says. "She'll figure things out."

Mom lays Kaylee on the changing table that we put in the living room.

"Boo," I say, trying to distract her while Mom takes off her diaper. Mom is fast at slipping a new diaper underneath her and fastening the tabs. "Why do some people like boys better in China?"

"Boys can work on the farm and help their parents. Girls get married and leave the home."

I think about Mom's sisters in China. One works in a bank and lives with Grandma Wai Po. The other teaches music in a nearby elementary school. "That's not true about girls anymore," I say.

"But some people don't change their thinking."

"Did your parents wish you were a boy?"

Mom snaps Kaylee's undershirt and pulls on her

sweatpants. "Nai Nai was a very modern person," Mom says. "She did not think like this."

"Anyway, I'm glad we adopted a girl."

"A boy is good too," Mom says.

"Laura and Camille and I are always talking about how lucky we are to be girls." Mom sets Kaylee on her feet. She toddles over to me and hugs me around my legs. "Girls . . . They hug more, and they talk more too."

"Not always," Mom says, handing me Kaylee's jacket. "My father used to hug me more than my mother did. And Ken talks so much."

I stuff Kaylee's arms into the sleeves, then pick her up and kiss her cheek. "I still think it's a good thing you're a girl."

Kaylee watches my mouth while I talk. Then she rubs her face in my sweater.

As soon as Mom buckles Kaylee into her car seat, she starts crying. I sing her the gumdrops song a bunch of times. Then we have to wait at the first intersection because of a train, and she starts whimpering again. Mom keeps looking at the clock.

"Look, Kaylee," I say. "A train. Choo-choo."

Kaylee stares out the window. Her cheeks look bigger than they used to, and she has a double chin. Maybe that means she gained weight.

"*Yi, er, san, si, wu,*" I say. "One, two, three, four, five trains."

Kaylee watches the train cars. Finally the caboose goes past and the wooden arm across the road goes up.

Three
Kaylee's Checkup

At the doctor's office, the nurse asks us to take Kaylee's clothes off and sit her on the scale. She screams as if we're killing her, because it's metal and freezing. Mom's mouth is in a thin, straight line as she waits for the digital display. Nineteen point four.

"Last time she was nineteen point two," Mom says, scooping Kaylee up and holding her against her chest.

The nurse puts a dot below the last line on the graph on the computer. "She is still below the fifth percentile for fifteen months." He turns to us. "Sometimes when babies come from orphanages, it takes them a little while to adjust." He stands up to leave. "The doctor will be in shortly."

"Shhh, Kaylee, it's okay now," Mom says. But Kaylee still cries.

If all the raindrops were lemon drops and gumdrops, oh how glad I'd be," I sing.

Kaylee gets quiet.

"Did they have a lot of food for the babies at the orphanage?" I ask.

"I think so, but we can't know for sure." Mom kisses Kaylee's cheek.

A lump grows in my throat. We don't know if Kaylee had sisters or brothers. We don't know if the family had enough to eat. We don't know what day she was born. We don't know anything except that somebody left her in front of an office building wrapped in a blanket and a lady who worked there found her and took her to an orphanage.

"Maybe she's just skinny like me," I say. "What percentile was I in?"

"You and Ken were both in the twenty-fifth."

"What does *percentile* mean?"

"That twenty-five percent of the babies your age were about the same weight as you," Mom says.

So that means that only five out of a hundred babies Kaylee's age are nineteen point four pounds and the rest are heavier. But when I look at her face, she doesn't look at all like the sickly babies I've seen in Mom's nursing journals.

We have to wait a long time for the doctor. Kaylee reaches for me. I walk her around the small room, singing to keep her quiet. When the doctor finally comes, Kaylee starts up again. The doctor looks in her ears and eyes and listens to her heart. I don't know how she can hear anything with all that screaming.

She reads the information on the computer and asks about the orphanage in China. "What were the conditions like?" she asks.

"Everything seemed fine," Mom says.

The doctor is typing while Mom talks. "Did the babies look like they were well fed?"

"Many of the other babies were chubby," Mom says. "But we did not actually go to the orphanage."

"Does Kaylee say any words yet?"

Mom looks at me. "I don't think so."

"Can she understand when you talk to her?"

"I'm not sure."

I feel as though the doctor is being kind of mean to Kaylee, like she's supposed to be chubby and she's not, and she's supposed to talk but she can't. "Sometimes she says 'ah ah ah' when we sing her the gumdrops song," I say.

The doctor doesn't type that.

"We have to keep working on Kaylee's weight," she says. "Bring her back in three weeks and we'll see how she's doing." The doctor makes some check marks on a piece of paper. "We want to make sure that she gains."

"She did gain a little," Mom says.

The doctor nods. "And keep talking to her." I don't like the way the doctor makes it seem as if we aren't taking care of Kaylee right.

"What should we do?" Mom asks. Her voice is thin and worried. A baby is crying in the next room.

"Try to get her to eat as much as possible." The doctor stands up. "And we'll see you back shortly."

Before we leave, the nurse comes in with a shot. I cringe because I hate shots, even the small allergy kind, and this one has a big fat needle.

"Just a little bee sting," he says to Kaylee.

Mom is holding Kaylee again. The nurse rubs her thigh with alcohol and sticks the needle in. Kaylee screams so long, she can hardly breathe.

"It's okay," I say, patting her head over and over. "It doesn't hurt anymore." I hold Mom's keys in front of her face. "Look, Kaylee." I jingle them.

Kaylee stares for a minute.

"*If all the raindrops were lemon drops and gumdrops,*" I sing.

Kaylee is listening.

"Seems you have the magic," the nurse says. He hands me the paper with the check marks. "Can you give this to the person at the front desk?"

I help Mom pull Kaylee's undershirt over her head. "We have to get her to eat more," Mom says.

"Look," I say, touching a wrinkle on Kaylee's thigh. "She's not that skinny. And look here." I point to the dimples on her feet, one for each toe.

"You heard what the doctor said." Mom pulls on Kaylee's pants and hands her to me.

"You're just fine, baby girl," I whisper into her cheek, which is wet with tears. I want to hurry and leave this office.

Kaylee falls asleep in her car seat.

"I don't like this doctor. Why can't we take Kaylee to my doctor?"

"She doesn't see babies under three anymore," Mom says.

"This doctor isn't very nice."

"She is trying to help us," Mom says, slowing down when she sees a yellow light.

"I really don't think Kaylee's that skinny. I mean, look at her cheeks."

"The doctor reads the numbers on the scale," Mom says.

"The scale doesn't show the wrinkles." I look over at Kaylee. Her head is leaning against the side of the car seat. She smiles in her sleep. "I think she's dreaming about China."

"Maybe."

"Do you think Kaylee has sisters and brothers in China?"

"It's possible," Mom says.

Thinking about Kaylee's first family makes me feel weird. I'm Kaylee's sister and Ken is her brother. We live at 2543 South Meadow Street in a brick house with four bedrooms. Her last name is Wang, just like ours. "What was Kaylee's name before we got her?" I ask.

"The man who brought her to us in the hotel called her Bao Bao. But the adoption papers just say *nv hai*, baby girl."

"No last name?"

Mom shakes her head.

"Was she in a box or something?"

"I'm not sure. I know she was wrapped in a blanket."

Suddenly I wish we still had that blanket instead of all the new pink ones. Kaylee would like it if we wrapped her in that blanket. Maybe then she would eat more and we wouldn't have to bring her to the doctor's office all the time.

Kaylee doesn't wake up when Mom puts her in her crib.

"I think we all need a nap," Mom says, pushing her hair back behind her ear. She has dark shadows underneath her eyes.

"I'm not tired," I say.

"Why don't you see if Laura is home?"

"She's at her dad's today." I follow Mom into her room. No matter how many questions I ask about Kaylee, I always think of new ones. "Did you pick

Kaylee off of a list of babies, or did they assign her to you?"

Mom lies down on her bed. "When we applied to adopt a baby, the government agency assigned her to us and told us the name of her orphanage."

"How did you decide to name her Kaylee?"

"Dad saw it in a baby name book. We thought it sounded so cute."

"You could have named her Bao Bao."

"That is a nickname for any baby, like Doll Baby. It is not a real name."

"You could have picked a Chinese name."

"Chinese is too hard for people to pronounce." Mom yawns. "Kaylee is easy to say."

Mom closes her eyes and I tiptoe out of the room.

Four
Naptime

$\mathcal{I}$ go into my room, sit down at my desk, and look at the homework listed in my planner. I already did the math problems and I finished *Because of Winn Dixie*, which I liked pretty much. The only thing left to figure out is what I'm going to do for the science fair. Ms. Henry, our science teacher, said they used to do the science fair only in sixth grade, but now they're extending it to fifth so we can get an early start on the scientific method.

We're supposed to start by making observations. Then we'll form a hypothesis, which is like a sort of prediction. We have to test our hypothesis and change it if we want. Finally we have to come up with some sort of conclusion.

I look out the window. The sun is shining behind dark gray clouds. That's an ob-servation, but what would my hypothesis be? It looks like rain, but that's an obvious prediction. Besides, what would I test?

Our house is so quiet when Kaylee is asleep. I can't believe it used to be like this all the time. She's been with us for less than three months, but it seems much longer to me. I still remember the exact minute when Mom and Dad told us that we were going to adopt a baby from China. We were sitting around the table after dinner, and Dad said he had some good news. Ken and I looked at each other. Ken thought maybe we were getting a trampoline, but Dad shook his head. I thought they'd finally agreed to let us get a kitten, but that wasn't it either. Then Mom said, "Dad and I are going to go to China." And Dad said, "To adopt a baby."

He explained how they'd always wanted more children, and been reading about orphanages in China that are overflowing with baby girls. He and Mom thought they should help. Ken got real quiet, but I asked a million questions, like what her name was and when she was arriving. Dad said they didn't have all the details yet, but our family had been approved relatively quickly.

That night, when I couldn't sleep, I kept trying to imagine our baby. Would she have big eyes like me or smaller ones like Ken? Would her hair be smooth and soft or sort of coarse like mine? Everyone says I look more like Dad and Ken looks more like Mom. But our new baby wouldn't look like any of us.

The next morning, I had run up the hill to Laura's. "You won't believe what my parents told us last night," I said as soon as she opened the door.

"Good or bad?"

"Great!"

"You're going to Disney World."

"Better."

"You're getting a trampoline."

I shook my head. "We're adopting a baby girl from China!"

Laura couldn't believe it. "Chinese babies are the cutest in the world," she said. "You are *so* lucky." We made plans to take the baby to the playground and fix her hair in ponytails and sew her little outfits.

Maow Maow comes in, stares at me, and jumps onto my bed. She flexes her claws in my bedspread and curls up for her afternoon nap. I could do my science fair about our cat. Observation: She flexes her claws before she goes to sleep. But what sort of a hypothesis would I come up with? I have no idea why cats do that.

I go over to the bed and pet her soft fur. We weren't planning to get a cat, but while Mom and Dad were in China getting Kaylee, Ms. Watkins up the  street found a cat in her garage. She couldn't keep it because her grandson is allergic. Grandma had come from California to stay with us, so she called my parents and they said that if there was absolutely nobody else who could take the cat, we could keep her for a while. Ms. Watkins brought her over, and she's been here ever since. Grandma called her Maow Maow, which sounds like "cat" in Chinese, and it stuck.

Maow Maow puts her head back so I can scratch underneath her chin. She purrs so loud, her whole body is shaking. I could try to find out why cats purr, but I only have Maow Maow and that wouldn't be enough for an experiment.

I look at all the books on my shelf. Ken used to be obsessed with dinosaurs, so we have *Dinosaurs Roamed the Earth, Dinosaur Alphabet,* and *Prehistoric Animals.* Then there are a bunch of picture books like *Little Blue and Little Yellow* and *The Little Engine That Could.* On the bottom shelf is my whole set of Laura Ingalls Wilder. When Dad read them to me at night, I dreamed of living on the prairie and doing everything ourselves, like hanging a door on its hinges and cutting wood for the stove. But I don't really feel like reading any of these little-kid books anymore.

If only Kaylee would hurry and wake up. Finally I hear a whimper coming from her room. I open the door, and as soon as she sees me, she stands up in her crib and holds out her arms. "Hi, Bao Bao," I say. I pick up my sister and smell her baby smell. She rubs her eyes with her fists the way she always does when she's sleepy. Then she opens her mouth and puts it on my cheek.

"Was that a kiss?" I ask.

Five

Worrying

When Ken comes home from Alan's, he says he wants pizza for dinner, not stir-fried chicken and green pepper with rice.

"We will have pizza another day," Mom says.

"Alan's allowed to eat whatever he wants for dinner," Ken says, pushing back his plate.

I glare at Ken to try to get him to stop complaining. Mom has enough to worry about with Kaylee not eating.

"Anyway, I'm not hungry," he says.

Kaylee keeps pointing to things on the table, but when we give them to her, she either bats them away or mashes them on her tray.

"She's still eating some," Dad says.

"Not enough," Mom says.

"We can't force her." Dad picks up a piece of chicken up off the floor and puts it into his napkin.

I don't really like chicken and green pepper either, but I eat everything on my plate.

After dinner, I help Mom give Kaylee her bath. While Mom goes to get Kaylee's towel and soap, I get her undressed. "Boo," I say when I pull off her shirt.

Kaylee stares at my face.

I cover my face with her shirt. "Boo," I say again.

Kaylee pulls at the shirt.

Mom runs the water, but when we put Kaylee into the tub, she starts crying.

"It's just water," I say, dripping some onto her stomach.

She reaches for me.

"Wait. You just got in." I wind up a plastic goldfish that flaps its tail and propels itself through the water.

"Look, Bao Bao."

Kaylee watches the fish.

"Look, I caught a fish," I say, holding the goldfish, which is still flapping.

Meanwhile, Mom rubs soap all over Kaylee and wets her hair. "Anna, put a little shampoo into my hand," she says.

I squeeze some out and Mom starts lathering Kaylee's hair. A little water drips into her eyes and she whimpers, but when I wind up the goldfish, she forgets all about it.

"Did I like baths when I was a baby?" I ask.

"You liked water from the minute you were born," Mom says. "But Ken didn't, remember? Unless I gave you two a bath together. Then he was okay."

I can't remember Ken being that little, but I do remember that he threw a fit every time we had to go to swimming lessons. I had to bribe him with promises to make paper airplanes for him when we got home just to get him into the car. I hear his voice downstairs, arguing with Dad.

"Ken is spoiled," I say.

"He was used to being the youngest," Mom says. I

squeeze more shampoo into her hand and she lathers Kaylee's hair a second time. "It's not easy to be in the middle all of a sudden."

It's not easy to be the oldest either, I think. Before we got Kaylee, Mom said we would repaint my room and change the wallpaper border, but now there's no time.

"I was in the middle," Mom says. "My older brothers bossed me a lot. And my youngest sister was the spoiled one. I think the middle is the hardest."

"The oldest one is supposed to be perfect all the time," I say, thinking about the way I cleaned my plate at dinner while Ken whined about wanting pizza. "And the oldest one has to take care of the rest of the kids."

Mom rinses Kaylee's hair. She looks worried, but she doesn't cry. "You can be the boss," Mom says. "Ken can't."

"Ken only listens when he feels like it."

That's how my brother has always been. He does what I tell him to when he wants to, but when he doesn't, he ignores me. Like yesterday, when I told him not to leave his socks all over the place and he walked right past them. And today, when I asked him to take Kaylee's smelly diaper out to the trash, he held his nose and ran outside, so of course I had to do it.

I wind the goldfish up again. "Still, the oldest one has more privileges," Mom says. "I used to be jealous because my older brothers were allowed to go out with their friends by themselves, but I had to stay at home."

Kaylee reaches for the fish.

"You'll see when you are older," Mom says. "You will be allowed to do things before Ken or Kaylee. Anyway, you are all three lucky not to be the only child. Your cousins in China have no brothers or sisters."

We went to China once when I was little, so I met Mom's family, but the only one I really remember is Wai Po. I know that each of Mom's siblings has one child because now that's all you're allowed to have in China. Even if Ken is spoiled, it would be boring to be the only kid in the family.

Mom takes Kaylee out of the water and wraps her in the towel. Then we lay her on Mom and Dad's bed to get her pajamas on. I pick up one of Mom's nursing

magazines that's on the nightstand. The first article is about breastfeeding.

I skim the first paragraph. "It says you should breast-feed for a year."

"Breast milk is very nutritious," Mom says.

"Was Kaylee breastfed?"

"We don't know." Mom is rubbing Kaylee's skin with baby lotion and she is trying to grab the bottle.

"We can call the orphanage and ask."

"Ask what?"

"If they have any more information about her."

"How can they find out?" Mom says. "A baby wrapped in a blanket . . . there is nothing to find out."

Mom puts Kaylee into her pajamas and I fasten the snaps down the front. She tries to grab my hands.

"Maybe the nurse weighed her wrong," I say.

"Doctors' scales are very accurate," Mom says.

"Maybe we should just stop worrying about it," I say.

Mom shakes her head. "No, Anna." The lines in Mom's forehead seem to be there all the time now. "Stop worrying and our baby will not eat."

Six

November Storm

Mom is holding Kaylee on her lap and reading her *Goodnight Moon*. Kaylee's eyes close for a minute, but as soon as Mom stops reading, she opens them again. Mom is getting so tired that she is almost asleep herself.

"I can read to her," I say, sitting in the rocking chair. Mom hands Kaylee to me and I smell the baby shampoo in her hair as she leans back against my chest. I open the book. "In the great green room there was a telephone and a red balloon." I turn the page. "And a picture of the cow jumping over the moon." Finally, when I get to "Goodnight nobody" and "goodnight mush," Kaylee's head flops down and she is asleep.

I wish I could just sit with her on my lap all night, but I know I would get too sleepy. I carry her over to the crib, lay her on the mattress, cover her with her pink blanket, and tiptoe out of the room.

I sit down at my desk and rummage around in the top desk drawer. There is my old drawstring bag from last year with a few old acorns inside, and a couple of markers and pencils. I close the drawer and look around my room. For my sixth birthday, Mom and Dad surprised me with the balloon wallpaper border. I loved to count the balloons as I fell asleep at night, but now it looks so babyish. And I'd like to paint the walls a pale green instead of this baby blue. Mom has every other weekend off from her nursing job at University Hospital, but she's exhausted by the time Kaylee's asleep. Dad has no time at all between his job and his night classes.

At least I can change my bulletin board. Last year, I covered it with pictures of kittens, but now that I have a real cat, I want something else. I take off all the old pictures.

I leave the bulletin board empty and get into bed.

The heater is hissing and I can hear the wind blowing the mulberry tree outside my window. Maybe I should read some, but Mom and Dad don't like me to stay up late. I close my eyes and see swirls of colors. I wonder if everyone sees colors like that behind their eyelids, or if some people see only black. I could do my science project about that. Observation: Some people see swirls of colors when their eyes are closed. But what would my hypothesis be?

A flash of lightning fills my room. If I were blind I couldn't see the light but I would still hear the thunder. Weather interests me, so I could do my science project about storms. But that's the kind of thing that needs all sorts of instruments, and Ms. Henry said we should do something that we can actually show. I turn onto my stomach and press my face into the pillow. It's strange to have a thunderstorm in November. Maybe Kaylee is scared all alone in her crib. I wish she'd snuggle here with me. We could make a tent out of the blanket with a little flap to peek out into the dark.

In the middle of the night, the thunder wakes Kaylee up. Mom and Dad take turns walking back and forth with her in the hallway. Dad sings the gumdrops song.

"If all the raindrops were lemon drops and gumdrops
Oh, how glad I'd be.
I'd sit outside with my mouth open wide
Ah aha ah aha ah aha ah—"
Then I hear something—Kaylee is trying to repeat *Ah aha ah,* but it sounds more like *Ahhhhhh.*

I go into the hallway. *"Ah aha ah aha ah aha ah,"* I say.

"Ah ha," she repeats.

We go back and forth like that until her eyes close again.

"Thanks," Dad whispers. Then he tiptoes into Kaylee's room and puts her back down in her crib.

I go back to my bed and look out the window. The rain has turned to drizzle, making a halo around the streetlamp. I wonder where Kaylee lived when she was first born. Did she sleep with siblings in one big bed? Or with her parents? If she were with them now, would she be a better eater?

Seven

Tug of War

In the morning, the sun is shining. Maow Maow is on the front porch with her fur all puffed up, hissing at our neighbor's cat. "Stop it," I say, smoothing her fur. "Smokey is your friend." She arches her back and Smokey takes off down the driveway. "You should try to be nice to the neighbors," I tell her.

Laura is coming down the street. "I thought you were at your dad's this weekend," I call out to her.

"He had to go someplace." She steps onto our porch and runs her hand down Maow Maow's back. "She's so pretty. I like all the colors."

"Me too." I rub the cat under her chin. Then she

goes to the door and stands up on her hind legs. I open it and we follow her in.

"What's her name again?" Laura asks.

"Maow Maow."

"Oh, yeah. That means 'cat' in Chinese, right?"

"Yup."

"So you named your cat Cat." Laura puts her jacket on the sofa. "We named our old cat Dog because he came when we called him just like dogs usually do. Dog Edwards." Laura sees Kaylee's highchair in the kitchen. "That's so cute," she says, touching the pink hearts painted on the back of the seat.

"Camille's mom gave it to us at the shower," I say.

"You're so lucky," Laura says. "I wish I had a baby sister. I hate being the youngest."

"It's not that great being the oldest," I say. "I have to help with Kaylee all the time."

"But that's fun."

"Most of the time. But not at the doctor's office."

"Do you have to go?" Laura sits down at the table.

I pour milk into two glasses, add big spoonfuls of

Nestle Quik, and heat them up in the microwave. "I'd feel bad if I stayed at home."

"Can't your mom get her to quiet down?"

"Kaylee does better with me." I set the two glasses on the table. "My mom's worried about her all the time."

"Why?" Laura asks.

"She's hardly gained any weight since we got her."

Laura looks at a picture of Kaylee on the refrigerator. "She looks fine to me."

"I know. But babies are supposed to gain weight."

Laura stirs her hot chocolate. "So what are you supposed to do? Force her to eat?"

"That's what I'm wondering."

We put our cups in the sink and go upstairs to my room. I take the sewing basket down off the shelf. "Remember when Mr. Shepherd gave this to us?"

"And we made all those fabric lunch bags," Laura says. "I still use mine. When I go to my dad's." Laura sorts through the buttons and safety pins. "I wish your

mom was still cleaning Mr. Shepherd's apartment. I liked going there with you guys."

"I kind of liked it too. Now that my mom's working at the hospital and we got Kaylee, we hardly ever have time to visit him."

Laura holds up an outgrown baby sock that's in the bottom of the basket. "I can't believe our feet used to be this small. I don't know if even Kaylee's feet can fit in here."

"Hey, let's make it into a little mouse," I say.

We stuff the sock with bits of rags and tie it tightly. Then we sew on pink buttons for eyes, cut felt ears, and tie a string to the tail.

I hear a *meow* and who is looking into the window but Maow Maow. "How did she get up here?" I ask. "I bet she climbed up the brick," Laura says. "Cats have really sharp claws."

I open the window and she jumps inside.

Kaylee toddles into my room. Her cheek has sleep wrinkles, and her hair is a mess.

"Your sister is so cute."

Kaylee holds on around my legs.

"She looks like you," Laura says.

"She's adopted."

"I know. But she still looks like you."

I don't know what to say. The only reason Laura thinks we look alike is because we're both Chinese. "Her nose is smaller," I say.

"I didn't say *exactly*," Laura jiggles the sock mouse in front of Kaylee. "Look."

Kaylee smiles and reaches for the mouse. Then she drags it into the hallway. From behind the door, Maow Maow pounces on the mouse.

"So now that someone else wants the mouse, you want it too," I say to the cat.

Kaylee pulls the mouse and Maow Maow keeps trying to get it. Finally she gets her paws all tangled up in the string. Kaylee gets a really intense look on her face and starts yanking the string.

"Tug of war," Laura says.

Kaylee pulls harder and the cat lets go.

Kaylee makes a funny sound deep in her throat.

"I think she's trying to laugh," I say.

The cat puts her nose in the air and walks out as if

to say *Who cares about a sock mouse and a bunch of girls anyway?*

Mom takes Kaylee down to have a snack. I find more small socks in our rag bag, and Laura and I make four more mice, two small ones and two medium.

"Now let's name them," Laura says. She holds the smallest one. "How about Ping."

I don't like that name. I don't know what to say.

"And the other ones could be Ming, Ling, or Ting. You know, like Quack, Mack, Flack in . . . What was it?"

"*Make Way for Ducklings,*" I smile now that I see why Laura thinks the names should rhyme.

Laura lines the mice up in a row. "They're so cute. Let's make up a story about them."

"Like the baby one gets lost," I say.

The phone rings and it's Laura's mom telling her it's time to go home. "I forgot, we're going to my brother's band concert this afternoon," Laura says.

"Do you have to go?" I ask. "You could ask if you could just stay over here."

"My mom says Andrew will feel bad if I'm not there."

She pulls the hood of her rain jacket up and heads down the street. When she's near the bottom of the hill she turns and waves. I wonder if she's going to her dad's tonight or not. I hope she isn't because I like knowing she's close by.

Eight

First Word

The phone rings. I bet it's Camille calling to see if we can review the math problems. She always gets nervous on Sunday nights because Monday is coming and she never feels ready.

"Hi, Anna. I'm calling to see how she's doing." The voice is familiar, but I don't know who it is.

"Who is this, please?"

"I'm sorry, I forgot to introduce myself. This is Ms. Watkins from up the street, the one who found the cat in my garage. How's she doing?"

"Just fine."

"That's what I thought. I wanted to check in."

"Thank you."

"Thank *you*, Anna. And thank your mom and dad again for me, okay? And Grandma, too."

I hang up, and suddenly Maow Maow pounces out of nowhere, grabs my leg, and claws me right through my jeans. "Ouch," I shout.

She scrambles into the den.

I pull up my jeans, and my ankle has a scratch.

Mom gets me an alcohol wipe. I cringe as I wait for the sting that I know will come. Kaylee is watching me clean the scratch. Then she toddles over to pick up the sock mouse on the floor, and holds it against her cheek.

"She really likes that mouse," Mom says.

Kaylee comes to me. She has her eyebrows pulled together and she looks very concerned as she bends down to inspect my ankle. Then she offers me her mouse.

I pick her up and kiss her cheek. "Thank you, Bao Bao," I say. "But you can keep the mouse. The scratch doesn't really hurt."

The mouse is dangling.

There is Maow Maow, crouching and moving her hind legs as she gets ready to pounce.

"That cat," Mom says, shaking her head.

Kaylee jerks the mouse back. "*No*," she says.

Mom's whole face lights up. "She said her first real word! We have to tell Dad! And the doctor."

"I can't believe she said it to the *cat*." I say.

In the middle of the night I wake up and realize that I forgot to study my spelling and vocabulary words. Last year in fourth grade, they were so easy that I got

100 without studying. But this year there are usually some words I don't know.

I turn on the light, rummage in my backpack for my notebook, and flip quickly through the pages. Twelve words this time: *hospitality, lively, simile, metaphor, insomnia, delicious, desert, dessert, adapt, superfluous, comprehensive, limerick.* I look hard at the words and spell them in my head. Then I close my eyes and try to remember as many as I can. I think of pictures to go with each word, like *desert* goes with camels and sand. In about ten minutes I have the words memorized. I turn the light off again and lie still in my bed.

Camille can hardly believe how I can memorize. "How do you do that?" she asks when we study together. I tell her it's kind of like taking a picture of words in my brain. Camille writes them over and over again and still she usually misses some. In Chinese school, she does better, but it takes her longer than it takes me to memorize the characters. "You're lucky," she always says. "You're smart." Lots of people tell me that. Laura said her mom said that Chinese people are smart. I wonder how that makes Camille feel when she gets 75s on her spelling tests.

I wish it were morning, because I'm not tired and the colors behind my eyelids are swirling like a funnel cloud. That reminds me, I still have no ideas for my science fair project. Ms. Henry said to think of things that genuinely interest us, things we really want to find out. She said we should pay attention to everything we can for a couple of weeks and keep a notebook full of

random thoughts and observations. I turn on my light again and reach for a piece of paper and a pencil.

Observations, I write across the top.

> My cat purrs when I pet her.
> She flexes her claws before she goes to sleep.
> I see colors when I close my eyes.
> They swirl when I rub my eyelids.

I hear Mom and Dad talking in soft voices downstairs. They're probably trying to figure out some way to get Kaylee to eat more.

> My baby sister doesn't eat enough.
> Girls are better than boys.

What else have I observed?

> Buckeyes sometimes come in groups of three.
> This November the weather is warmer than usual.

But none of these observations is going to turn into a science fair project.

Nine

Our Natural World

My classroom is really noisy. I look around, and
there is a substitute—again. My stomach turns over.
It seems like Ms. Simmons—Ms. Sylvester now that
she's married—has been absent a lot this year, and
the substitutes can never control our class. Three boys
are doing karate kicks in the back. Laura, Camille,
Allison, and Lucy are talking in the corner.

The substitute hits a ruler on the desk and for a
minute everyone is quiet. "Boys and girls, the bell has
rung. Take your seats."

The talking starts again as the kids move slowly toward their desks. I am between Ryan and Lucy. Camille
is two rows behind me and Laura is two rows ahead.

The substitute says we will start with math, and then we'll have our spelling test. Her voice is mousy and I can hardly hear what she's saying. Doesn't she know that a substitute has to be really loud? Even louder than Ms. Sylvester, and we can hear her voice through the closed door.

The spelling test is easy and I finish the fill-in-the-blank part early. I wish I would have brought a book to read.

Finally the substitute collects the tests and it's time to go to science in Ms. Henry's room. Allison and Lucy are walking on either side of Camille, who is much taller than the rest of us. She sees me. "Hi, Anna," she says with her wide-open smile. "I didn't see you this morning."

"I was almost late," I say.

When Camille first came to North Fairmount at the beginning of this year, I was the only one who already knew her since she's in my Chinese class on Saturdays, and her mom and my mom are friends. Everybody asked me if she was my cousin because we're the only two Asian kids in our grade, except for one other girl who's only half. I showed Camille where the gym was and the lunchroom, and the secret mound behind the tetherball where Laura and I say there is a man breathing under the dirt.

Ms. Henry hands out a packet to each of us called "Science Fair." Now that we've made random observations, we have to narrow things down and figure out what sort of projects we want to pursue. We will go to the library this morning to get ideas from books. We can work with a partner or in a small group.

In the library, everybody is looking around, trying to figure out who to work with and what to do. Ms. Henry says this first library visit is just for brainstorming. We don't have to settle on a topic right away. In fact, she says it's better not to settle on a project too quickly. Sometimes one thing leads to the next.

Camille looks upset. "What should we do?" she asks.

"We don't have to decide today," I say.

"I know, but should we do weather or plants or what?" Camille is always worried about anything related to school.

I pull a book off the shelf about tornadoes and we start looking at the funnel clouds. When I was little, there was a tornado that came through our neighborhood. All the way until about third grade, I was scared every time there was even a little thunderstorm. Then, finally, I got used to storms and even came to like them.

Laura looks at the pictures with us. "Can I work with you guys?" she asks.

I nod. "But we don't know what we're going to do."

"I know. But when you decide, can I be in your group?"

"Sure," Camille says. She's like that, always ready to include everybody in everything.

Lucy and Allison bring a book to our table called *Our Natural World: Science Fair Experiments*. "We've decided," Allison says.

"What?" asks Laura.

"We're doing plants. I mean, they're all around us."

"And I *love* flowers," Lucy says.

"Do you guys want to do it with us?"

Camille's face lights up. "I like flowers," she says.

"Me, too," Laura says.

Allison opens the book. "We can do this experiment about how plants absorb different colors. Okay, Lucy, in the section called 'Plant Nutrition,' you read the first chapter. I'll read the second. Laura, you read the third, and Camille, you can read the fourth one. Anna, you can do the last chapter and the appendix."

I look down. I don't really want to do a science fair

project straight from a book. Ms. Henry said we should use books to get ideas, not to copy from. Wouldn't copying an experiment from a book be sort of like reading a mystery when you already know the ending?

"I'm not sure," I say to Allison.

Ten

An Accident

$\mathcal{D}$ad is holding Kaylee and waiting for Mom to get home so he can make it to his accounting class on time. He keeps looking at his watch and pacing in front of the window.

"I can take care of her," I say.

Dad hesitates.

"Yeah, we can take care of her," Ken says.

"It'll just be for a few minutes," I say.

Kaylee squirms to get down. She toddles over to me, holds her arms out, and I swing her onto my hip.

Dad looks at his watch again. "Okay. Just play with her here in the living room, and Mom will be home any minute."

As soon as Dad leaves, Kaylee starts fussing. I sing her the gumdrops song, and she listens, but when I stop, she whimpers and struggles to get down. I set her on her feet and she goes to the window.

"Look at this, Kaylee." Ken does a cartwheel.

Kaylee watches.

Ken does another one, better than the first.

Kaylee smiles.

"She likes it," Ken says. "Now watch this."

He steps back to do a roundoff. When he lands, his foot hits the cocktail table in front of the sofa and knocks the candy bowl onto the floor. It shatters and spews glass and candy all over the place. Ken stands in the middle of the broken glass like a statue.

"Are you okay?" I ask.

"It was an accident," Ken whispers.

Kaylee is staring at the candy. She starts to toddle toward it, but I grab her. "No," I shout.

She starts crying.

"Go get the broom," I order Ken.

For a change, Ken does exactly what I tell him. He steps carefully between the pieces of glass and gets the broom from the closet. Then he tries to sweep the glass and candy into a pile, but instead he spews it all over the place.

"Not like that," I say.

"I'm trying," he says, choking up.

"Here. You hold Kaylee and let me sweep." I hand the baby to him.

The door opens and Mom steps into the living room. She sees the broken glass and scattered candy on the floor. "What is going on here? Where is Dad?"

"He went to his class."

"He left you three alone?" She shakes her head and mumbles something in Chinese that I don't understand. Then she takes Kaylee from Ken and carries her up to her crib. I follow behind.

"I told Dad we could watch her for a few minutes," I say, feeling my throat swell. "It was just an accident."

"Go get the vacuum cleaner." Mom's voice is deep. Kaylee is standing up in her crib, watching us, but she doesn't cry.

"I told Dad I could watch her because I can," I say. My voice is getting louder as I talk. "I am almost eleven years old, and I know how to take care of a baby." I swallow. "You always want me to help with Kaylee, and now that I did, you are mad." My throat is scratchy but I will not let myself cry.

Mom hurries out of the room and I hear her footsteps go down to the basement to get the vacuum cleaner. I know she is thinking that I am a girl who does not listen to her parents, a disobedient American girl with a loud voice.

I hear Mom turn on the vacuum cleaner. She runs it forever until there can't possibly be any slivers of glass. Kaylee lies down on her mattress and sucks her thumb. I lean over her crib and pat her head. "It's okay, Bao Bao. It's not your fault." She is staring across the room. "You are the best Bao Bao in the whole world—did you know that?" I rub her back until her eyes close. Mom turns off the vacuum cleaner and our house is quiet.

I go into my room and sit down at my desk. I bet Mom is mopping the floor now, just to make sure there's not a single speck of glass. She's always so careful about everything, especially if it's related to Kaylee.

I take a piece of scrap paper and start doodling. I could do my science fair project about parents and kids. Or I could do something about oldest kids, middle kids, and youngest kids. But it would take hundreds of kids to try to prove anything. And what about only children like Camille and my cousins in China? Or what about kids who are adopted? Would that make a difference?

I write WANG in all kinds of different letters, like shadow writing and block letters. Then I write the Chinese character for our name on the side of the page. It's so simple, two lines across, one down, and one more on the bottom. It means "king" in Chinese and it looks sort of like a crown. Maybe I could do my science project about Chinese characters and how some of them resemble pictures. But that would be a history project, not a science one. Plus, I know people have studied that before.

王

I write my first name, Anna, in curlicue writing. I always notice how different people have different ways of writing. Laura's handwriting is big and round and she dots her "i's" with circles. Camille's handwriting is small and perfect. But I cannot think of a hypothesis about handwriting.

❊ ❊ ❊

At eight thirty, I go to bed and fall asleep without even reading. But in the middle of the night I hear voices coming from downstairs. I sit up to listen. Mom is shouting, then Dad, then Mom. I can hear some of what they're saying but not every word. Something about responsibility and baby and thriving. I know Mom is blaming Dad because he left us alone with Kaylee. But it was my idea, not his. Maybe I should go downstairs and tell Mom that I wanted to take care of my baby sister. But she might be mad that I am awake.

Then I hear a sound coming from Kaylee's room. She's not crying or whimpering. I sit up so I can hear better. Her voice is going up and down. Could she be trying to sing?

Maybe Kaylee remembers a song from the orphanage. Or maybe her first mom sang it to her.

Later, I hear Mom get up and go into the bathroom to get ready for work. Nurses have to go to work at all kinds of odd times.

When my alarm rings in the morning, I feel like I could sleep forever.

Eleven

Science Fair

$\mathcal{I}$'m standing on the curb, waiting for Ray the crossing guard to stop the cars. It's starting to drizzle and the wind is strong. "Cold front's coming," Ray says, looking up at the clouds.

Allison runs up. "Hey, Anna, are you coming over after school?" She pulls her hat down over her ears.

"What for?"

"Did Lucy forget to tell you? To plan our experiment."

Ray moves into the intersection and Ken rushes across. "Hurry, girls," Ray says. "It's cold this morning."

Ray is right. I wish I had worn my warmer jacket.

"My mom said she'd pick us up," Allison says. "I have all the books at my house."

I really don't want to do the experiment from the natural world book, but I don't know what to tell Allison. "I'm not sure," I say, hurrying into the school building.

Ms. Sylvester says she was not at all pleased with our last spelling tests. We have to remember that we are in fifth grade, which means we are ten or eleven years old and it's time to buckle down if we want to be ready for middle school next year. Her face looks really disappointed. I got 100 on my test, so I know she's not talking to me, but still I wish she was happy like she was last year. When fourth grade ended, I was so glad that Ms. Sylvester would loop with us, but now she is irritable a lot of the time.

"Write one sentence for each new spelling word," she says.

"Can we write a story with the words?" I ask. "Or does it have to be separate sentences?"

"A story is fine," she says.

"Can we change the words a little, like *nourishment* instead of *nourish*?"

"Yes, Anna," she says. Her face looks annoyed, as if she is tired of my questions.

I look at the list again: *plagiarism, nourish, strength, definitely, awkward, lifelong, situation, precocious, conscience*. Then I start writing:

In China there was a baby girl whose parents were so poor that she didn't get enough nourishment. Her strength wasn't great, but she was a precocious baby. The parents had a lot of daughters and they definitely wanted a son, so they put their baby daughter in front of an office building where somebody would be sure to find her. This situation bothered their conscience lifelong, but there was nothing they could do. The other sisters asked about the baby, and the parents answered awkwardly. Finally when one of the sisters grew up, she decided to search for her lost sister.

This story is not plagiarism.

I wish I could throw my paper away and start over. I don't want Ms. Sylvester to read it, because she might think it's true. But I don't have time to write new sentences, so I put my paper into the basket on her desk.

After we turn our papers in, we are supposed to work on our science fair projects in the back of the room. "Thanksgiving break is coming," Ms. Sylvester says, "and by the time you come back, you should all have a solid start."

Allison is sitting at the table with her notebook open. "Here's the task list," she says. "Everyone can pick what they want to do."

Lucy and Laura join us. Laura says she'll put in the food coloring. Allison takes a red marker and puts her name next to that task. Lucy says she thinks her mom will take

Task List

1. Get bulbs.
2. Get food coloring (at least 3 colors).
3. Get containers.
4. Put in the food coloring.
5. Observe the flowers.
6. Record observations.
7. Draw a conclusion

her to get the dye and the containers, so Allison marks that down too.

"I think we're supposed to do the observation part first," I say.

"That's not what the book said." Allison is holding the marker. "So which part do you want, Anna?" She's standing with one foot in front of the other, waiting. "You could get the bulbs."

I take a deep breath. "I think I might do something else."

"Like what?" Laura asks.

"I like animals better than plants," I say.

"I like animals too," Laura says. "But it's hard to do an experiment with them."

"You can't hurt them or anything," Lucy warns.

I know they are right. Plants are easier. And it's nice of Allison to try to organize everything and to include me. But I don't want to do this project about plants in dye that's probably been done thousands of times. The pictures in the book show each step. You put the bulbs in the water with different food coloring and watch how it affects the blossoms. But we already know that the flowers turn colors from the dye in the water. The only thing for us to really observe is how dark or light the colors are.

"Well, the world can't live without plants," Allison says. "They're the basis of all life." She sighs. "So, are you going to do your own science fair project?"

I don't know what to say. I really don't want to do something all by myself, but I don't want to use an experiment from a book. I want to do something where I don't know how it will turn out . . . something that really matters. "I'm not sure."

"When are you going to decide?" Allison's voice is sharp.

I glance around the room. Camille is the only one still working on her spelling word sentences. Her head is close to the paper and she is gripping her pencil really hard.

"You guys can go ahead without me," I say.

Allison looks at Laura and Lucy. "Who wants to get the bulbs?"

Lucy says she will.

"And who wants to record the observations?"

"Camille has really nice handwriting," Laura says.

Allison takes a blue marker and writes "Camille" with a fancy *C*.

I can change my mind. I can tell them that I will get the bulbs or record observations. But all the tasks are already assigned. I open my notebook and write Science Fair in big cursive letters. I make designs all around the page.

Ms. Sylvester is walking around the room. When she gets to Allison's group, she says "Sounds very colorful. Make sure you take pictures of the flowers."

For some reason, I feel a lump grow in my throat. Last year Ms. Sylvester liked me a lot. But now she is tired of me and sometimes I am tired of her, too. She comes around the side of my table.

"Any ideas?"

I shake my head.

Ms. Sylvester goes over to the shelf and pulls out a book. "Why don't you take a look at this." The title of the book is *Maps of the Ancient World*. "Maybe it'll trigger something for you."

The cover of the book looks interesting, but I don't know how it could help me with my science fair project. The bell rings and it's time for lunch.

Twelve

A Surprise

There's lots of traffic because people are picking up their kids to go out of town for the holiday. Ken and Alan are up ahead, laughing and pretending to shoot baskets. I make my way around them. On Thanksgiving Day, we'll have a big dinner at Camille's house with all the other Chinese families like we do every year. Only this time, Kaylee will be with us. It will be fun to show her off to all the aunties. Auntie Linda will make my favorite roasted duck.

Laura comes up behind me. She's kicking a soggy sweet gum ball and not saying much. "Are you going to Michigan?" I ask.

"I don't know," she says. "My dad wants us to spend Thanksgiving at his house, and my mom wants us to go to Michigan, and Andrew and David want to go to a beach in Florida." Laura kicks the sweet gum ball into the street.

"I was thinking that if you're home, we could sew a dress for Kaylee."

Laura's face lights up. "I think my mom has some material with little cats all over it that would be perfect."

A car slows down and it's Laura's dad. He stops and opens the window. "Hop in," he says.

"Where are we going?" Laura asks.

Her brothers are in the back seat. "To my apartment," he says. He smiles. "You guys are spending Thanksgiving with me."

Laura looks at me. "I'll call you as soon as I get home," she says, getting into the car.

When I get home, Dad is holding Kaylee and stirring something on the stove. Ken is making faces to get her to laugh.

"Guess what?" he says. "Grandma is coming from San Francisco!"

"When?"

"Tonight!" Ken jumps and shouts so loud that Kaylee gets startled.

I can hardly believe it. Every year we hope Grandma will come from California for Thanksgiving, but she usually can't because she has to take care of her sister. "What about Auntie Wendy?" I ask.

"She's living in a retirement home now, so she'll be well taken care of." Dad turns off the stove. "It was a last-minute idea. We were able to get her a standby ticket."

"How long can she stay?" I'm already thinking of how Grandma can help me sew Kaylee's dress.

"We're not sure. We'll see how it goes."

"How what goes?"

"How Kaylee does," Dad says. "Mom took her back to the doctor, and she lost half a pound. The doctor was really concerned."

"So is that why Grandma's coming?" I ask.

Dad blows on the oatmeal. "Partly." He puts Kaylee into her highchair and spoons a little bit of oatmeal into a pink plastic bowl.

"How can Grandma make Kaylee eat any more than we can?"

"We'll just have to see, Anna," Dad says.

Kaylee stares at the spoon with a stubborn look on her face. I get a spoon of my own and put some oatmeal into my mouth. "Mmm, good," I say.

Kaylee watches me. Finally she opens her mouth and Dad gets a little in. Most of it comes out onto her bib. But maybe she swallows something.

When Mom and Dad went to China to get Kaylee, Grandma stayed with us for three weeks. She showed us how to crochet little worms to use as book markers and how to cut carrots into flower shapes. She made seaweed soup for dinner, which I loved, and in the evening we played gin rummy. I hope she'll stay for a long time.

After our snack, I go up to my room and take the book from Ms. Sylvester out of my backpack. It's full of ancient maps with intricate borders and words I cannot understand. It seems as if some of the mapmakers thought the world was flat. They had no idea where the continents really were or the oceans or anything. I like the pictures, but why does Ms. Sylvester think these maps could possibly help me come up with an idea for my science project?

I get a cup of water, open my small tray of watercolors, and start to copy one of the maps of China with the paintbrush. I add the mountains in brown and the rivers in blue. Our Chinese teacher tells us about different parts of China, and she shows us paintings and calligraphy. Maybe someday I can go with Kaylee and we can visit Wai Po and our aunts and uncles and cousins in Shanghai.

I blow on my painting, and on the top I write "To Grandma" in red paint. Then I take it up to the attic and put it on Grandma's bed.

Thirteen

Grandma Arrives

Mom is at work at the hospital. Dad and Ken and I have a quick dinner of pot stickers from the package. Kaylee watches us eat, but when Dad tries to give her some, she bats it away.

Ken clears the table and I wash the dishes while Dad gets Kaylee ready. Grandma's flight arrives at eight thirty, and it's already eight. We're about to leave for the airport when Kaylee poops. I don't see how she can eat so little and poop so much. We have to take off her jacket and all her clothes and change her diaper. It's almost eight fifteen, so Dad drives fast. Ken and I hold on to the handles above the windows and hope the police don't stop us.

By the time we park and make our way inside, Grandma is already there. Ken and I run to hug her.

"You've both grown about a foot," Grandma says, holding us close, so I can smell the anise that I love. "And I think I've shrunk a foot."

"Sorry we're late," Dad says, hugging his mother and holding Kaylee at the same time.

"No problem at all." Grandma touches Kaylee's cheek. "How is our little one?"

"She lost a half a pound," I say.

"Yes, Dad told me," Grandma says. "But she still looks bigger than when I saw her in September."

Kaylee holds up the little mouse.

"And who gave you this?" Grandma asks Kaylee.

"Laura and I made it," I say.

"How is your new cat doing?" Grandma asks as we head to the baggage claim.

"She's not what I'd call friendly," Ken says.

"Cats always act like they don't need us," Grandma says. "When inside they do."

"How do we know they need us?" Ken asks.

"Little things. Like they'll bring you a dead bird."

Then Ken tells Grandma about how he won the Lego contest at school, but she is talking to Dad about Kaylee and how she brought some special nutritional herbs from Chinatown. She doesn't even know Ken is talking to her. When he notices, he gets quiet.

"Who got second place?" I ask Ken.

"Alan."

"What did he build?"

"A robot. But it looked pretty much like the picture that came with the set."

"What did you make?"

Ken smiles. "A multicolored cat!"

"Really? Do you still have it?"

"I had to take it apart after the contest. But Ms. Sylvester took a picture of it."

Ken describes his Lego cat, how he made the ears pointed with the smallest pieces, and he used some wire that came with the robot set to make whiskers. I love the way he talks with his hands when he's excited. Even if Dad and Grandma aren't interested in Lego building, I am.

Dad pulls into our driveway, and the cat is sitting right on the front steps.

Grandma laughs. "She's waiting for us."

"I don't know," I say. "She has her eyes closed."

"So does Kaylee," Grandma says.

I pick Kaylee up gently so she won't wake up, and carry her across the yard.

"She dropped her mouse," Ken says. The cat dashes over but Ken grabs it first. "Hey," he says. "I thought you were asleep."

Grandma laughs. "Seems there is some kind of contest going on here."

Fourteen
Camille's Idea

When I wake up, the sun is high and it's almost ten o'clock. I can't believe I slept so long. I wash my face with cold water and go downstairs. Everyone is crowded into our kitchen. Mom is making rice-covered meatballs to take to Auntie Linda's for Thanksgiving. Grandma is cooking baby food for Kaylee with the special herbs. Ken is throwing his newest paper airplane around the kitchen. Kaylee is banging lids together like cymbals. Maow Maow is lurking behind the door.

Ken runs to answer the phone. "It's Camille," he calls.

"I'm not in Lucy and Allison's group anymore." Camille's voice is matter-of-fact. "My mom told me to ask you if we could work together, but I know sometimes you like to do things . . . I mean, you have your own ideas." She takes a deep breath. "But can you help me?"

That's how Camille is, always ready to move forward.

"Do you know what you want to do your experiment on?" I ask.

"That's the problem. I'm trying to figure out a topic."

"Me, too."

"We're supposed to decide before we go back to school," Camille says.

Suddenly I want to see Camille's open face. Maybe together we can come up with something. "Can you come over?"

Camille and I sit on the floor of my room. She looks around. "How do you know how to make so much stuff?"

"I'm not really sure. My grandma taught me how to

sew doll clothes when I was little. Next she's going to show me how to crochet."

Camille picks up my old cloth lunch bag. "I like this." Then she sees the family of sock mice.

"Laura and I made them," I explain.

"Laura didn't come to the meeting at Allison's."

"She was probably at her dad's. So, did Allison just kick you out of the group?"

Camille arranges the mice into a circle. "Everybody was supposed to do a certain task. Allison and Lucy thought I should make the science fair board because I have nice handwriting. But I don't want to do just the writing."

"Did you tell them?"

"I said that first I wanted to understand how flowers get water up from the roots. I mean, water doesn't usually flow *up*." Camille is opening and shutting the drawstring bag. "But Allison said that didn't matter for our project because it's about dye, not water. Plus she knows I can't read very well."

"So what happened?"

"Allison said that maybe it would be best if I found another group. She was pretty nice about it, really." Camille swallows. "I guess she's right. It takes me a long time to read stuff. And the group can't wait forever."

"I think that's mean," I say. "Is Laura still doing the project with them?"

"I don't know. She wasn't there, so it seems like Lucy and Allison are doing everything by themselves." Camille winds the drawstring around her fingers. "Now I don't know what to do."

"Me, either."

"You always think of things," Camille says.

"Not always."

"My mom says that ideas usually come when you're not looking for them. She says it's like when you're looking for something, you never find it." Camille puts her hair behind her ears. "So maybe what we should do is stop trying to think of a science fair idea."

I take the sewing basket off the shelf. "Want to help me clean it out?"

Camille lines the spools of thread up in a neat row.

I fold the fabric scraps. Kaylee is crying downstairs. I tell Camille what the doctor said about Kaylee not gaining weight, and how my grandmother is here now.

"That's good," she says.

"My grandmother can't make her eat."

"Maybe she can." Camille takes the safety pins and links them into a chain. "When my parents were worried because I couldn't learn to read, my grandpa helped."

"How?"

"Mostly he just read me a lot of stories. And he told my parents to stop bugging me to read signs and menus and stuff every second."

"Did that help?"

Camille looks down. "I still don't read very fast. But I can read."

"The doctor said that Kaylee isn't thriving."

"What's 'thriving' mean?"

"I guess it's like growing and talking and doing all the stuff babies are supposed to do."

Camille is really listening. "My mom says I didn't do stuff I was supposed to do either."

"Like what?"

"Like I never crawled." Camille smiles. "My mom even got down on all fours to show me how. But I just sat there."

"So how'd you get around?"

"I scooted. Until I started walking."

"You walk pretty well now," I say, thinking of how I have trouble keeping up with Camille's long strides.

"I might go out for the track team next year, if I pass to middle school, that is." Camille shuts the lid of the sewing basket with everything neatly organized inside.

I smile at her. "Of course you'll pass."

Fifteen

Thanksgiving Dinner

$\mathcal{I}$ like the smell of Camille's house and the sound of Chinese and English mixed together. Everybody is talking and laughing and passing Baby Kaylee around. For a while, she doesn't seem to mind all the commotion, but then she gets fussy.

"Can Camille and I take her?" I ask.

"She hasn't eaten yet," Mom says.

"Please."

Mom looks at Grandma and hands Kaylee to me.

I carry her downstairs and sit her on the rug. We put lots of toys around her from when Camille was little, like blocks and dolls and rattles. But what she's really interested in is Camille's hamster. She stands up, gets her balance, and toddles over. The hamster, named Mister, wiggles its nose, and Kaylee smiles. Camille takes Kaylee's hand and helps her pet Mister's thick fur.

Camille shows me her reading corner. "This is where my grandpa read to me for hours." She takes a book off the shelf. "I loved this one," she says. *Chinese Folk Tales and Nursery songs.* Camille starts reading them in English and in Chinese.

"Wow, you're really good at Chinese," I say.

"I just memorized these songs and poems," she says. "My grandpa read them to me so many times that they got stuck in my head."

Kaylee comes over and sits between us.

Camille sings a nursery rhyme in Chinese about fruit: *"shui guo shui guo zhen hao chi."*

Kaylee listens.

"She likes it," I say. "I wonder if she understands some Chinese."

Camille puts her face close to Kaylee's. *"Ni hao, xiao mei mei,"* she says. Hello, little sister.

"In the orphanage, they called her Bao Bao."

"*Ni hao, Bao Bao,*" Camille says.

Kaylee stares blankly and reaches for the book.

Camille is smoothing Kaylee's hair. "How about at meals, you sing her the Chinese poems. To help her forget about eating." She looks at the armchair where she read with her Grandpa. "I forgot that I couldn't read when Grandpa read to me."

Kaylee bangs on the book. Camille reads her another poem. Kaylee lies down on the carpet and closes her eyes.

"She looks so peaceful," Camille says.

I play with the carpet fuzz and think about how Camille is always trying to help other people. But then other people don't always try to help her. "Allison isn't very nice."

Camille is quiet for a minute. "When I am with her by herself, she's different."

"What do you mean?"

"The other day she was sitting alone in the locker room, and she told me that her mom's always nagging her."

"About what?"

"About her clothes and her hair. Her mom wants her to go to modeling school so she can learn how to carry herself."

"What does that mean, 'carry herself'?"

Camille shrugs, then pats Kaylee's hair. "Sometimes I think we're lucky we're Chinese. I mean, if Allison weren't blond and skinny, I don't think her mom would be . . . I don't know how to explain it."

"What about when David and Robert pull their eyes and say 'Ching chang chung'?"

Camille sighs. "I hate that."

"Or when Laura names the little sock mice Ming, Ping, and Ling."

Camille raises her eyebrows. "What's wrong with that?"

"It just sounds so . . . Chinese. I mean, she could have said they were Ashley, Jason, and Max."

Camille considers this. "My cousin in China is named Kai Ming and we call him Ming Ming. Anyway, Laura's nice."

The smell of food is making me hungry. "Dinner must be ready," I say.

Camille takes a deep sniff. "I hope so."

I pick Kaylee up carefully, trying not to wake her up, but she opens her eyes. I kiss her warm cheek and we go upstairs.

Auntie Linda's duck is juicy and tender. But Kaylee won't even put a little piece into her mouth. She fusses and mashes her food around with her hands.

"Let me try," Grandma says, shoving a spoonful of rice with meat into Kaylee's mouth.

Kaylee spits it out.

Camille gets up, stands by Kaylee's highchair, and starts singing one of the Chinese songs from the book. Her voice is strong and clear. Kaylee sits very still and listens. Everyone else gets quiet too.

Slowly the corners of her mouth turn up. Camille puts a small piece of duck into Kaylee's mouth and keeps singing. Kaylee chews it and swallows. She eats three small pieces of duck before she starts batting it away.

On the way home, Kaylee falls asleep in her car seat. Ken says she's drooling on him and he wants to switch seats with me.

"Just move your arm over," I say.

"She's still drooling," he says.

"It won't kill you," I say.

"Stop bickering," Mom says. "Maybe since it's Thanksgiving, we should think about what we're thankful for."

"I am not thankful for baby spit," Ken says.

"Ken," Mom says sharply.

We are quiet after that. I remember last year Ms. Sylvester asked us to write what we were thankful for, and I said the mini cereal boxes that I like so much. This year if she asks us, maybe I'll write that I am thankful for my two best friends. I'll draw a picture of three buckeyes in one shell and label them Camille, Laura, and Anna.

Kaylee stretches, opens her eyes for a minute, and then closes them again. Or maybe I'll draw a map of China and an airplane. Underneath it I'll write 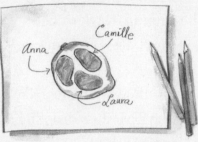 that I'm thankful we adopted Kaylee. But thinking that makes me feel strange, because even though we've only had her for three months, I can't imagine our family without her. We have a picture from last Christmas with Mom and Dad in front of our house, and me and Ken sitting in a pile of leaves. It looks wrong to me now. I want to take a new picture with Kaylee in it. And Maow Maow, too, if we can get her to sit still long enough to snap a picture.

Before her bath, Mom weighs Kaylee and she hasn't gained at all.

"At least she didn't lose," Dad says.

"She ate some duck," I say.

Mom seems like she doesn't hear us.

"I bet the scale's wrong," Ken says. "It could be broken."

Mom takes off Kaylee's clothes and puts her into the bath water.

"Look, the wrinkles on her thighs are deeper," I say, rubbing soap on her legs.

"That's hard to measure," Mom says.

I'm tired of worrying about Kaylee's weight. I stand up and dry my hands on the towel. Mom can give Kaylee a bath by herself.

I go downstairs and sit down at the computer. I know Camille said we should stop trying to think of a science fair project, but we really do have to come up with something. I put "science fair fifth grade" into Google, and there are lots of sites full of projects. I click on one about growing beans, but even the pictures are boring. I click on another about food groups and a third about music and memory. Nothing gives me any ideas.

Then I put "baby not thriving" into Google. Wikipedia has a long entry about it with charts that show how babies are supposed to grow. I scan the article. Near the end it says that sometimes babies who are not thriving have to be hospitalized. They may need IV hydration and a feeding tube.

I click off the site and stare at the blue screen with lots of small icons. The Internet can be great, but I don't ever want to look at that site again.

Sixteen

Groups of Girls

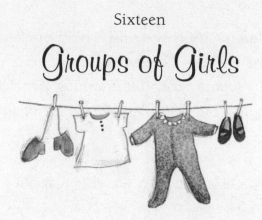

Thanksgiving break is over and Ms. Sylvester is absent again. This time we have the building sub, Ms. Lamar. She puts the agenda for the day on the board and tells us to work quietly at our desks.

Spelling word sentences
Math problems
Sustained silent reading
Science fair

I don't even try to make a story with the spelling words. I just want to hurry up and finish. The math problems are pretty easy, and I have everything done in forty-five minutes. Now what?

I was in such a rush this morning that I left my book at home. But Camille passes me a book with a note.

My grandfather sent me this book and I really liked it.

The cover is red and it has a picture of a girl's hair on the cover. I read the flap and I can't believe there's actually a whole book about two Asian girls. One is ABC, American-born Chinese, like me, and the other one just came from China. I've read fifty pages when the bell rings for lunch.

The weather is warm for December, so Ms. Lamar gives us extra recess. Laura and Camille and I go behind the building to our mound.

"Why'd you guys think there was someone buried under here?" Camille asks.

"See the cracks in the dirt?" Laura says. "They keep

getting bigger. And when you stand on the mound and shut your eyes, you feel yourself going up and down."

Allison and Lucy are coming toward us. "Ms. Sylvester's not coming back until after Christmas," Lucy says.

"How do you know?" I ask.

"I heard Ms. Robinson talking to the sub," Allison says.

"Is she sick?" I ask.

"I don't know. She just asked the sub to stay until January. By the way," Allison says, looking at Laura, "we started our experiment. We put the bulbs into different colored water. Our next meeting is Tuesday after school."

"I can't come Tuesday," Laura says quickly.

"Why not?" Allison asks. "I mean, the plants can't wait forever."

"I'm at my dad's on Tuesdays," Laura says. "Remember?"

The wind is strong. Allison's skirt blows up and we can see her pink underwear. She grabs her skirt and pulls it down. "I hope nobody saw that," she says, roll-

ing her eyes and giggling. Then she looks over at Robert and David, who are watching her. She grabs Lucy's
arm and they head toward the boys.

"They're mean," I say.

"Allison called me last night," Camille says. "She said
she was sorry for asking me to find another group."

"Did she ask you if you wanted to come back?"

Camille nods. "But I said I couldn't because I was
doing something with you." Camille looks at me.

"I think I want to leave their group too," Laura whispers. "Can I join yours?"

"We don't have a project yet, but maybe between the three of us, we'll come up with an idea!" Camille says.

Then Laura says she has a stomachache.

Camille takes her hand. "I get stomachaches when I'm too hungry. I have an apple in my desk."

I follow behind. Camille is talking to Laura, telling her how much she likes the little sock mice we made. Laura is smiling. Camille really is good at helping people with their problems, even if sometimes it just means getting them to think of something else.

By the end of the day, I finish the book Camille lent me. The two girls in the story don't even want to be friends at first because everyone thinks they're supposed to like each other just because they're both Chinese. But it ends up that they really do like each other. I want to re-read this book. It seems as if it was written just for me.

Seventeen

Finally!

When I get home, Mom is at work and Dad is in class. Ken went over to David's after school. Grandma is there with Kaylee, trying to spoon a mashed-up banana into her mouth. As soon as the spoon gets close to her lips, Kaylee squeezes them shut and gets her stubborn look.

Grandma sets the spoon down. Her face seems older, with deep lines around her eyes.

"Maybe she's not hungry," I say.

"She's hardly had anything to eat all day," Grandma replies.

Kaylee looks like she's about ready to cry. I start

singing the gumdrops song, and she listens. When I get to the *Ah aha ah* part, she tries to join in.

Grandma starts singing it too.

I cut a slice of banana and put it into Kaylee's hand. Slowly she moves it to her mouth. We keep singing the song over and over again without stopping. Kaylee eats three slices of banana.

"Thank you, Anna," Grandma whispers.

"It was Camille's idea," I say, remembering how Camille sang to Kaylee at Thanksgiving.

Grandma wipes Kaylee's face with a washcloth, takes her out of the highchair, and stands her on her feet. She wobbles for a minute, and then toddles toward her sock mouse, which is on the counter. Maow Maow is glaring from the corner.

"That cat and Kaylee are two peas in a pod," Grandma says. "They both like mice, they both eat very little, and they're both stubborn."

Kaylee comes to me and holds up her arms until I pick her up. "There is one difference," I say.

"What's that?"

"Kaylee wants me to hold her and the cat doesn't."

"I had a cat once who wouldn't come out of the basement for a year," Grandma says.

"And then what?"

"One day I found her on the sofa in the living room, lounging in the sun." Grandma washes Kaylee's high-chair and the floor around it. "Oh, Anna, I forgot to thank you for the lovely painting you gave me. Now, was that a map of China?"

I tell Grandma about the book Ms. Sylvester lent me with the ancient maps. "She said it might help me get ideas for my science project. So far it hasn't, though."

"But it gave you ideas for your painting." Grandma smiles.

I go up to my room. I don't feel like doing my home-work, so I start looking through a box of old pictures inside my desk. There is one of our family sitting on the sofa the day after Ken was born. He's a little lump in Mom's arms, and I'm trying to touch his bald head. Then there's one of me when I'm about two, holding the hose and watering the grass. I start pinning them on the bulletin board like a collage. We don't have any pictures of Kaylee when she was born, but we have the one Dad took on the day they left the hotel. Kaylee is holding the blanket in one hand and Mom's hand in the other. I put that picture in the middle of the collage.

I read through my list of random observations for the science fair project. I can't think of anything else to add. I doodle on the paper, making curly designs around the border. Maow Maow jumps onto my desk and sits right on top of the ancient maps book. "Move," I say, pulling the book out from underneath her. She settles back in the spot where the book was.

Some of the old maps look nothing like the real thing. One has California like an island, and another one has India next to Africa. I wonder how they could even begin to figure stuff out without satellites and airplanes. Maybe they just guessed. That's what a hypothesis is. You observe something, you guess about the reasons, and then you test it to see if it's true. I hear Grandma downstairs washing dishes and singing to Kaylee.

Suddenly I know what our experiment could be.

I call Camille, and in fifteen minutes, she is at the front door.

Eighteen

Bananas and Hamburgers

𝒫roblem: I write on the paper. *Kaylee needs to gain weight.*

Observation: Kaylee does not want to eat enough. She throws food onto the floor. She spits food out after she chews it.

Hypothesis: She eats more if we sing songs while she eats.

Materials: Kaylee and her food.

Camille reads the paper silently. Then her whole

face turns into a smile. "It's so real," she says. "I mean, it's not just a science fair project. How'd you think of that?"

"It was your idea," I say.

"It was my idea to sing songs to your sister, but not for a science project."

"That was my part," I say, grabbing her hand.

Camille thinks we should test different songs. "Maybe Kaylee likes Chinese songs better than English ones."

"We could try two English songs and two Chinese songs," I suggest.

"But how are we going to know which ones she likes better?"

"We can count how many slices of banana she eats."

"Maybe we should try other food too," Camille says.

"I think bananas are enough. Or it'll get too complicated."

Camille considers. "I don't think so. I mean, she might get tired of bananas and start hating them."

I like the way Camille says what she thinks, even if other people don't agree. "We could cut up little pieces of my mom's Chinese hamburgers. They're so good, nobody could ever get tired of them."

"This science fair is making me hungry," Camille says.

We go down to the kitchen and Grandma steams us bean paste *bao zi* for a snack.

"Let's call Laura," I say. "She loves *bao zi*."

"Mind reader," Laura says when she hears my voice on the phone. "I was about to come over anyway."

Laura puts her jacket on the chair and takes a deep breath. "Your house always smells so good."

"Especially when my grandma is here," I say.

Grandma gives us small plates with two *bao zi* each. I take the first bite. "Perfect," I say, tasting the sweetness of the hot bean paste.

Camille tells Laura about Kaylee and our science fair idea. "Do you want to do it with us?"

Laura finishes her first *bao zi*. "Allison didn't exactly kick me out of the group, so I don't know what to tell her."

Camille has her eyes closed like she does when she is thinking hard. "Just say that you can't meet on Tuesdays because you're at your dad's, and their project is almost done."

Laura nods. "That's the truth. I think they almost finished the whole thing already." She looks at my notebook, open on the table, and reads our notes. "This is really cool. I mean, it's not just for the science fair."

"It's for Kaylee," Camille says.

"But there's one thing," Laura says. "How can we tell if she gained weight?"

"We'll just have to go with her to the doctor," I say. "They have those baby scales that are really accurate."

"Do you think your mom will let all of us go?" Laura asks.

I ask Grandma.

"If it's for the science fair," she says, "I don't think Mom will mind."

❄ ❄ ❄

After Kaylee's nap, we sit her in her highchair and slice a banana. Then we stand around her and sing the gumdrops song.

Kaylee finishes one slice. *"Ah aha ah aha ah,"* she says.

We sing the song again, and she eats two more slices. We want to see how much she'll eat with the Chinese fruit song, but she is reaching for me to take her out of the chair. "She's already full," I say, wiping her mouth and her hands.

We go up to my room to plan out our project. "Maybe we should try one song each day," Laura says.

I nod. "Because when a baby's full, they won't eat no matter what."

"How about 'Twinkle Twinkle' for one of the English songs," Laura says.

"And the gumdrops song," I say.

Camille makes a list:

Twinkle Twinkle Little Star
Gumdrops

"We can ask Teacher Zhen which would be the best Chinese songs. She has two little kids, so she probably knows," Camille says.

For now she writes:

Chinese song 1
Chinese song 2

"So for food, we could use bananas and my mom's Chinese hamburgers," I say.

Camille writes that. "I think we should try each song on more than one day."

"Yeah. And maybe we should have one column with

no songs at all," Laura suggests. "So we can see if the songs really do make a difference."

Camille adds that to the list. "Do you have a big piece of paper so we can make a graph?"

In my closet I find a poster that I made for Earth Day last year. The back is blank, so we use that. Laura and Camille are good at measuring out the columns, making everything look very neat.

While they work on the columns, I write the introduction:

In China there are many baby girls to adopt because some people like boys better. They can only have one child because the population is too big. My parents wanted to give a baby a home, so they went to China to adopt Kaylee. When she got to the United States, the doctor said she was too thin and that maybe she wasn't thriving, so we were supposed to get her to eat more. The problem was, she's stubborn and she wouldn't eat.

Then we noticed that she liked songs and poems, so we decided to see if she would eat more if we sang songs to her. We also want to see if she eats more with Chinese songs or English songs.

Laura reads what I wrote. "I like it," she says. "But Ms. Henry said we should make everything very clear."

"I think it is clear," I say.

Laura takes a piece of paper and writes *Observation* across the top. "I think we should list our observations about Kaylee."

We start listing everything we can think of:

1. Kaylee walks.
2. She says a few words but she doesn't really talk.
3. In her three months in the U.S., she lost a half of a pound.
4. She has rosy cheeks and wrinkles on her thighs.
5. She has dimples on her feet and hands.

6. She loves her sock mouse.
7. She follows the cat.

"She's the cutest baby in the world," Laura says.

"I don't think we can put that as an observation," I say.

"Why not?" Laura asks. "It's true."

"But some people wouldn't agree. I mean, you can't measure that."

"It's still my observation," Laura says.

Camille is considering. "How about put something cute that she does."

"Okay. She hugs Anna around her legs," Laura says. "And she fights with the cat."

Laura writes all that down.

"Now we have to state the hypothesis," I say. On another piece of paper I write:

Kaylee eats more when she isn't
thinking about eating, so we will sing her
songs to distract her, two in Chinese
and two in English. Then we will see if she

gains weight and we will see which songs she likes best and test two foods.

"Now we just have to wait to collect the data," Laura says.

Camille shuts her eyes for a minute. "I hope that when the science fair is over, Kaylee will be the healthiest baby in the world."

When Mom comes home from work, Grandma is holding Kaylee in the rocking chair. Kaylee looks like she's asleep, but every time Grandma stops rocking, she opens her eyes again.

I tell Mom about our science fair project. She sits at the kitchen table and listen to all the details. "Do you think we can go with you to Kaylee's next checkup?" I ask.

"All three of you?"

I nod. "It's part of our project."

"I'll call the office to make sure. But I don't see why not."

Kaylee's head flops forward.

Grandma stands up very slowly, carries her over to the sofa, and lays her down. Kaylee stretches but she doesn't wake up. Then she smiles in her sleep.

"She's dreaming again," I say.

"Maybe this time she's dreaming about banana slices," Grandma says.

Nineteen

Collecting Data

When we go to Chinese class on Saturday, we ask Teacher Zhen about Chinese children's songs.

"The fruit song is very popular," she says. Camille and I already know it because we learned it in class, but she teaches us two more verses. She says she will write out the words with the pronunciation in English letters so it will be easier for Laura to remember them. Then she teaches us a Chinese song about two tigers. "That one is my son's favorite."

"Maybe Kaylee heard those songs in the orphanage," Camille says.

"That is very likely," Teacher Zhen says.

❋ ❋ ❋

Camille can't come over on Thursdays because she has tutoring. Laura can't come on Tuesdays because she's at her dad's. I thought we could start our experiment over winter break, but Camille's family goes to visit her aunt in North Carolina and Laura goes to Michigan. We spend Christmas at home, reading and playing games.

At her checkup last week, Kaylee's weight was only up three tenths of a pound. According to the doctor, such a small amount is not really significant.

"What should we do?" Mom asked again.

The doctor kept looking at the computer instead of at Kaylee or at Mom. "Just keep working on it," she said finally, putting the weight into Kaylee's record.

Finally in January, Camille and Laura come over and we really get started on the experiment. I slice up a banana and put it on Kaylee's tray. The three of us stand around her highchair and sing the gumdrops song. Kaylee smiles and waves her arms. Then she eats three banana slices in a row.

"That's pretty good," Laura says.

"For Kaylee, it's great," I say.

Camille writes down the data: January 5: gum-drops song, 3 slices.

We do the same thing for ten straight days, using banana slices and different songs. On the days that Laura or Camille can't come over, two of us do the experiment, and each day one of us records the results:

banana data
January 5, Gumdrops song,
3 slices

January 5:
   Gumdrops song, 3
      banana slices

January 6:
   Gumdrops song,
4 banana slices

January 7: Fruit song, 4 banana slices

January 8: Fruit song, 4 banana slices

January 9: Tiger song, 6 banana slices

January 10: Tiger song, 4 banana slices

January 11: Twinkle Twinkle Little Star, 2 banana slices

January 12: Twinkle Twinkle Little Star, 3 banana slices

January 13: No song, no banana slices

January 14: No song, no banana slices

Then we do the same thing with pieces of Chinese hamburgers.

January 15: Gumdrops song, 2 pieces of hamburger

January 16: Gumdrops song 4 pieces of hamburger

January 17: Fruit song, 6 pieces of hamburger

January 18: Fruit song, 2 pieces of hamburger

January 19: Tiger song, 6 pieces of hamburger

January 20: Tiger song, 4 pieces of hamburger

January 21: Twinkle Twinkle Little Star, 4 pieces of hamburger

January 22: Twinkle Twinkle Little Star, 2 pieces of hamburger

January 23: No song, 2 pieces of hamburger

January 24: No song, no pieces of hamburger

Then we figure out the averages for each food and each song and make a bar graph to show our results.

Do Songs Help a Baby Eat?

HAMBURGERS AND BANANAS

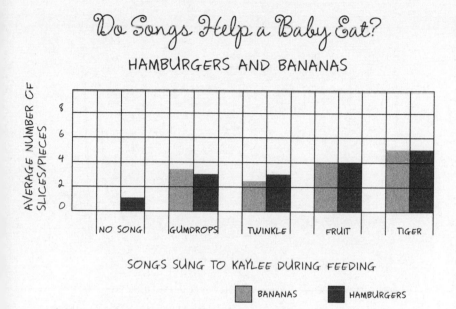

SONGS SUNG TO KAYLEE DURING FEEDING

BANANAS   HAMBURGERS

"The tiger song wins," Camille says, "with both bananas and hamburgers."

"And 'no song' loses," I say, "with both bananas and hamburgers."

We put the information on a big science fair board with pictures of Kaylee. I write Kaylee on top, and then I write Wang in Chinese characters.

Kaylee sits on the floor, watching us. Then she points to the pictures of herself. "Bao Bao," she says.

I kiss her cheek. "Now you're really talking."

Laura picks up the marker and writes "Bao Bao" next to Wang.

Laura's mom calls and says it's time for her to go home.

"We're almost done," she says. "Can I stay a little longer?"

But her mom says they have to go to her brother's basketball game.

"I'll write the conclusion," Camille says, sitting at my desk.

I know it will take her a long time, but that's okay. We don't have to take our boards to school until Monday.

I sit on the floor and play with Kaylee and the family of sock mice while Camille writes.

When she's done, she hands me her paper.

When I was in first grade, I could not learn to read. My parents were worried, so they asked my grandfather to come and help. He read stories to me that I liked, and then I learned to read when I forgot about how hard it was. I thought the same thing might be true for Anna's baby sister, Kaylee, who was adopted from China. When she doesn't think about eating, she eats more. She seems to like Chinese songs best, maybe because she heard Chinese songs in the orphanage before she was adopted by the Wang family. Her favorite song is the one about tigers. Her least favorite time to eat is when she has no songs to listen to.

I really like the simple way that Camille writes. She doesn't try to change anything or hide anything. "It's great," I say.

Camille looks down. "I'm not very good at writing with style."

"But everything you write is so true."

"There's one thing I left out," she says, pushing her bangs out of her eyes. "We can't really finish our project until we go to the doctor with Kaylee. Then we can see what the scale shows."

"She has an appointment tomorrow at two," I say. "And my mom said we can all go."

Twenty

A Crowd at the Doctor's Office

Kaylee is not as fussy in the car as she usually is. Camille makes funny faces to distract her, and Laura brings a CD with little kids' songs on it that we play pretty loud. But in the waiting room, she starts crying, and no matter what we do, she won't stop.

"She's afraid of shots," I tell Laura and Camille.

"I still cry when I have to get a shot," Laura says.

"But she's not getting any shots today, is she?" Camille asks.

"I don't think so. But she doesn't know that. Plus she hates sitting on that freezing scale."

"Kaylee Wang," the receptionist calls.

We follow Mom into the exam room. "Wow, quite a crowd today," the nurse says. "A Girl Scout troop?"

"A science fair group," Mom says. She looks at us. "Can you girls explain your project to the nurse?"

I take a deep breath. "We were worried about Kaylee, because the doctor says maybe she's not thriving. So we thought of a way to get her to eat more."

The nurse sits down on the stool. Kaylee has stopped crying and is staring at the cats on the wallpaper.

"We decided to sing Kaylee songs while she eats," Camille says.

"In English and Chinese," Laura says.

The nurse is really listening. "Well, let's see how Kaylee's doing, and we'll see if your songs did the trick," he says.

Kaylee whimpers when we get her undressed, but at least she's not screaming. When we sit her on the scale she reaches for me.

"Just a minute, Bao Bao."

Mom turns away as the nurse watches the digital display.

"Twenty point three." He smiles. "Up almost one pound!"

"YES!" Laura and Camille and I shout at once. I grab Kaylee off the scale and hug her. "You did it, Bao Bao. *Hen hao!* Very good!"

Kaylee makes a sound from deep in her throat.

"What was that?" Camille asks.

"She's laughing," I say.

When the doctor comes in, she is very pleased with Kaylee's weight gain. "Much improved!" she says, patting Kaylee's head.

"The girls want to tell you about their science fair project," the nurse says.

I start by explaining how Camille thought Kaylee would eat more if we sang her songs. Camille tells about how doing this for the science fair was my idea. And Laura describes the steps with the bananas, hamburgers, and songs.

"You know, this is something other people might benefit from," the doctor says. "We tend to worry so much that we forget things like songs and distraction as part of healing." She stands to go. "Would you mind sending me a summary of your project when you're done?" Then she shakes Mom's hand. "And congratulations. I'll see you back in two months."

"Isn't that a little long?" Mom asks.

"We can always reschedule if you have a concern. But I think two months will be just fine." Then she turns to us. "I really do want to thank you girls," she says. "You've reminded me that sometimes doctors forget that there is more to patients than numbers."

Kaylee is pointing to the wall. "Ca," she says.

"I think she's saying cat!" Camille says, pointing to the cats on the wallpaper.

"Cat," Laura says very clearly.

"Ca," Kaylee repeats.

"What a talker," the doctor says.

On the way home, Mom stops in front of the ice cream store. "I think we need to celebrate!" she says, turning off the engine. "After all, it's because of you three that Kaylee is doing better."

"What flavor does Kaylee like?" Camille asks.

"I don't know," I say.

"We can each get a different flavor and let her try them," Laura suggests.

Laura gets blackberry, Camille gets double chocolate, Mom gets peach, and I get pumpkin. Kaylee wrinkles her nose with blackberry and pumpkin. It seems she kind of likes peach. But with the double chocolate, she laughs. "Mo," she says to Camille.

"What?" Camille asks.

Kaylee reaches for the cone. "Mo."

"She wants *more*," I say, watching Kaylee's mouth open like a little bird's.

"Now your sister knows four words," Laura says. "No, *Bao Bao, cat,* and *more*."

"And she learned two of them today!"

Twenty-One

Science and Sewing

At school the next day, Ms. Sylvester and Ms. Henry are at a conference, but the sub tells us to set the science fair boards up in the room because the teachers may come in over the weekend to review our work. Then she gives us time to go around and look at everyone's boards.

David and Robert did their project about skateboard ramps. Their hypothesis was that the steeper the ramp, the faster you go, and the higher you can jump, which turned out to be true. Tai and Anthony did something to see if heavy backpacks make people shrink, and they don't. Lucy and Allison's hypothesis was that if you watered bulbs with colored water, the colors would go through the stems and into the flowers. They took lots of pictures of their flowers as they grew, and it turned out that the blue food coloring worked best, and the red second best. Their board is very pretty with drawings of bulbs and photos of plants around the border.

Lucy is looking at our board. "When I was a baby, my mom said I was a really picky eater."

"Really?"

"The only thing I would eat was pears."

"Did the doctor say you weren't thriving?"

"I don't think so." Lucy goes on to look at the next board.

For a second I wonder if we hadn't adopted Kaylee, if she were a biological sibling, then maybe the doctor wouldn't have even worried about her weight.

After school, Camille says, "I'm kind of sad we're done with the science fair. I like going to your house and singing songs to Kaylee."

"Me, too," Laura says.

"You guys can keep coming. And we can keep singing," I say. "I don't want Kaylee to stop eating just because our science fair project is done."

"She might get tired of it," Camille says.

"Maybe we can learn some new songs," I say. "Can you call your mom and see if you can come over?"

Ken and his friends are up ahead. Laura, Camille, and I lock arms as we walk. "It smells like spring," Laura says, taking a deep breath. "I can't believe it's not even February yet."

"Look," I say, pointing to green shoots sticking out of the ground. "I think those are daffodils."

"And crocuses," Laura says, pointing to small bright yellow flowers by the oak tree.

I unzip my jacket. "I'm actually hot."

"We forgot to plant the buckeyes we collected," Camille says. She turns to Laura. "Do you still have them?"

"I dumped them into a box. They're probably some-where in my room. I'll check, and if I find them, I'll bring them when I come."

As soon as we open the door, we can smell Grandma's soup.

Camille takes a deep sniff. "Chicken soup?"

"With long noodles," Grandma says. "For a long life." She gives us each a small bowl of soup and porcelain spoons.

"Did you girls remember that today is a holiday?"

I look at Camille. "Chinese New Year!" we say at the same time.

Grandma has four red envelopes for us with chocolate coins inside, one for Ken, one for Camille, one for Kaylee, and one for me.

"Thank you," Camille says. "I can't believe we almost forgot."

"And Teacher Zhen even reminded us last Saturday."

There is a knock at the door, and Laura is there. "My mom said the buckeyes got moldy so she threw them out. But I found this." She holds up the cat fabric.

"Would you like some soup?" Grandma asks.

"Yes, please." Grandma fills her bowl with hot broth and noodles. "I like these spoons." Laura takes a spoonful of the soup, blows on it, and puts it into her mouth. "And I love the soup."

"I have something else for you," Grandma says, handing her a red envelope with her name on the flap.

Laura looks at the ceiling like she is trying to remember something. *"Xin nian kuai le,"* she says slowly. Her tones are kind of flat, but we know she said "Happy New Year."

"Xin nian kuai le to you too," Grandma says.

Grandma helps us lay out the dress pattern pieces on the cat fabric. We cut carefully on the lines, then pin the pieces together and take turns sewing the seams.

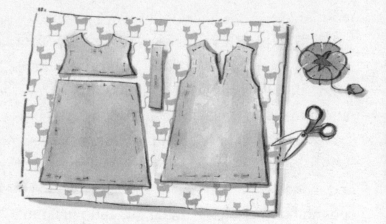

"Hey, listen," Camille says, stopping the sewing machine.

I hear Kaylee's voice from down the hall. Her soft voice is going up and down. "She's trying to sing the fruit song," I say.

We go into Kaylee's room and she's sitting in her crib, playing with her toes and trying to sing "*shui guo, shui guo, zhen hao chi.*" She sees us, smiles, and puts out her arms. "Up," she says.

The dress is more complicated than we thought. The straps get a little bit bunchy and Grandma has to redo the yoke. But finally it's finished and we try it on Kaylee.

"A little big," Laura says.

"She'll grow into it," Grandma says.

"Now that she's gaining weight," Camille says.

"Look, Kaylee," I say, pointing to her reflection in the mirror.

"See the cats?" Laura points to the print on the bib.

Kaylee stares at the cats for a minute. Then she turns

around like she's trying to dance. Camille thinks it's the funniest thing she has ever seen. Soon the three of us are laughing so hard, we can hardly breathe. Kaylee looks at us as if to say *What's so funny?*

Twenty-Two

Unexpected Visitors

When I wake up in the morning, my room is strangely bright. I look outside and snow is covering everything. I can't believe we are having a snowstorm and it's almost March. I bet Laura is sledding already. Then I remember, she's probably at her dad's.

Ken is trying to fit his feet into his boots, but he says they hurt.

"You can wear my old ones," I say.

He rolls his eyes. "They're pink."

"Do you want to go out or not?"

He puts the pink boots on. I get my new green ones and my jacket, scarf, hat, and mittens. Finally we're all set when Kaylee starts crying.

"She wants to go too," Mom says.

Ken grabs my sleeve. "Come on."

"It'll just take a minute to get her ready," I say.

"You two go out and I'll bring Kaylee," Mom says.

I follow my brother into the snow.

"Let's make a snowman," Ken says, starting with a small ball.

The snow is wet and sticks together. Ken makes the bottom ball and I make the other two. Together we stack them on top of each other. We use sweet gum

balls for the eyes, acorns for the buttons, and sticks for the nose and arms.

Kaylee is so bundled up that she can hardly walk. At first she's not happy about the snow on her boots and she tries to dust them off with her mittens. But then she sees the cat leaping around and forgets all about the snow.

Mom gets the camera and takes pictures of us three.

Finally my hands are frozen and Ken is hungry, so we go in.

"Ms. Sylvester called," Dad says.

The blood rushes to my face. My teacher has never called our house before. "What did she want?"

"She said she was so impressed with your science project. She wants you to enter it in the city-wide competition."

"So she called for that?"

"She asked if she and her husband could come over to talk to us. They might want to adopt a baby from China. And they'd like to ask us some questions," Dad says.

I cannot imagine Ms. Sylvester with a Chinese baby. But then Salina in my Chinese class is Chinese but her parents aren't, and Robert in my class is from Ethiopia but his mom and dad are from Norway.

"When are they coming?"

Mom and Grandma get busy making *bao zi* for Ms. and Mr. Sylvester, who will arrive in an hour.

"Maybe they don't like Chinese food," I say.

"If they're going to China to adopt a baby, they might like to try it," Mom says, handing me a circle of the floury dough. I squeeze it in my palm, put a little bean paste in the middle, and twist it shut.

I've never heard Ms. Sylvester's voice so quiet. She almost doesn't sound like herself. And she's wearing blue jeans and a sweater instead of her usual skirts. First she says how much she enjoyed the science fair project that Camille and Laura and I did.

"Thank you," I say. "It was Camille's idea. I mean, to sing to Kaylee."

"I'm sure the three of you worked together," Ms. Sylvester says.

"How is the baby doing now?" Mr. Sylvester asks.

"Better." Mom smiles.

"I saw in Anna's conclusion that she gained almost a pound. That's wonderful."

Grandma brings out the steaming hot *bao zi,* and Mr. and Ms. Sylvester each take one.

"Fantastic," Mr. Sylvester says, patting his belly, which is kind of large. "We'll have to try making these at home. If you'll give us a lesson, that is."

Then Ms. Sylvester says they've been having some problems having a baby, and they've decided that they would like to adopt a girl from China. They ask Mom and Dad all about the process and how long it takes, how much it costs, and how to get started. "Did you like the orphanage where you got Kaylee?" Ms. Sylvester asks.

"We didn't see the orphanage, but the babies seemed well taken care of," Dad says.

Mom looks at her watch. "Anna, please check on Kaylee. She's been asleep for a while."

❊ ❊ ❊

On my way up the stairs, I hear Kaylee. When I peek into the room, she is sitting up in her crib and talking to Maow Maow, who is crouched on the dresser. Both of them are looking at the sock mouse in Kaylee's crib.

"Mine," Kaylee says with her eyebrows pulled together.

The cat jumps off the dresser and follows us.

I carry Kaylee downstairs and set her on the floor. Mr. and Mrs. Sylvester cannot take their eyes off her.

"She doesn't look too thin to me," Ms. Sylvester says.

"I'd say she's pretty near perfect," Mr. Sylvester says.

I sit on the floor next to Kaylee and smooth down her hair. I know nobody's perfect, but I wouldn't want my sister to be any different from exactly the way she is.

"She drools all the time," Ken says.

"Only when she's getting new teeth," Mom says.

Kaylee is talking to her mouse.

"Is she talking in Chinese?" Mr. Sylvester asks.

"Just baby talk," Mom says.

"Was it difficult for her to adjust?" Mr. Sylvester asks. "I mean, her life must be so different here from in China."

Mom looks at Dad. "It's hard to tell with a baby."

Mr. Sylvester shakes his head. "Her birth parents must miss her."

Mom looks down. "I think so."

Dad gives the Sylvesters some websites to help them get started.

"Do you think we'll be able to get our baby this summer?" Ms. Sylvester asks.

"I'm not sure," Dad says. "I hear it's taking longer to adopt babies these days."

"We'd better get started then." Mr. Sylvester takes a second *bao zi*.

Mom says it might be hard to do everything in China if you don't speak Chinese. "Maybe I should go along to help," she suggests.

"We wouldn't want to impose on you," Ms. Sylvester says.

"No problem," Mom says. "Actually, I want to go

back. I want to try to visit the orphanage. Now that I know Kaylee, I have so many questions." Mom is quiet for a minute.

"Like what?" I ask.

"I wonder what her favorite foods were."

"And her favorite songs," I say.

"And there's something else. I just really want to thank them for what they did for us," Mom says.

I try to imagine Mom and me and Mr. and Ms. Sylvester in China. Suddenly I really want to know what it looks like and smells like and who the people are. "Can I go with you?" I ask.

Dad looks at Mom. "I don't know, Anna. The tickets are very expensive."

"Anna would be a big help to us," Ms. Sylvester says.

"We can pay for the ticket," Mr. Sylvester says. "Anna knows Chinese and knows about babies. What more could we want?"

"What about me?" Ken asks.

"We will play lots of gin rummy," Grandma says. "And you can teach me to build with Legos."

Suddenly the cat pounces on Kaylee's mouse. She pulls it away. The cat walks off like *So what, I wasn't trying to get it anyway.* Ms. Sylvester laughs.

When Mr. and Ms. Sylvester get up to leave, they tell us that they have registered for Chinese classes.

"Where?" Mom asks.

"Over at the church on Spalding Road," Ms. Sylvester says. "They have a beginner's level."

"That's the same place we go," I say. "Ken is in level two, and Camille and I are in level three."

"You must speak very well," Mr. Sylvester says.

"Is there a class for adults?" I ask.

Mr. Sylvester shakes his head. "We'll be right in there with the kids. Good practice for being a parent, right?"

"Laura's in that class," I say. "Maybe she can help you."

Grandma wraps up the four leftover *bao zi* and gives them to Ms. Sylvester. I pick Kaylee up to say goodbye. "Say bye-bye."

Kaylee waves by moving her fingers. Then I notice that she is holding a *bao zi* in her other hand, and there is a small bite missing.

Steamed Red Bean Bao Zi

yields 16 buns

1 tablespoon (1 packet) active dry yeast

1 cup warm water, plus additional as needed

4 cups all-purpose flour

2 tablespoons granulated sugar, divided

1 teaspoon double-acting baking powder

1 teaspoon kosher salt

Filling: red bean paste (available at an Asian food store)

Materials needed: parchment paper, oil spray, towel, steamer

1. In a small bowl, sprinkle the yeast over the warm water. Allow to proof, or set, until bubbly, about 10 minutes.

2. Put the flour, sugar, and baking powder into a bowl and mix. Add the salt and pour in the warm water-yeast mixture. Mix until the dough begins to form a ball. If it looks too dry, add more water, tablespoon by tablespoon, until it forms a ragged clump. Turn the dough out onto a floured countertop and knead by hand until the dough is smooth and shiny.

3. Place the dough in a well-oiled bowl and flip it to coat in oil. Cover with plastic wrap and store in a warm, draft-free place until the dough doubles in size, approximately 2 to 3 hours.

4. Cut 16 squares (approximately three inches each) of wax or parchment paper. Spray each square with cooking oil.

5. Punch the dough down, then divide in half. Roll each half into a log. Slice each log into 8 pieces. Roll a slice into a ball, then shape it into a thin, flat disk (like a pancake). Try to keep the center of the disk thicker than the edges.

6. Spoon a dollop of bean paste filling into the center of the disk. Pull the edges up around the filling and pinch together to form a bun. Place the bun on a square of parchment paper and cover with a towel. Continue this process with the rest of the dough until all of the buns are filled. Allow the buns to rest for 20 to 30 minutes.

7. Working in batches, position filled buns (each still on its parchment square!) into a steamer, allowing room on all sides. (The cooked buns will be up to 50 percent larger.)

8. Steam the buns for 15 minutes, then remove the pan and basket from the heat. Let sit for 5 minutes

before removing the lid. Remove the parchment paper from the bottom of the buns and serve immediately.

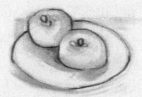

The Year of the Fortune Cookie

Follow Anna Wang to middle school in the third book in this series, *The Year of the Fortune Cookie*. Anna travels to China to help her teacher adopt a baby girl, but she worries: Will she really be able to contribute? And will she really be able to help the babies at the Lucky Family Orphanage? And how will it feel to be in a place where everyone is Chinese?

With the help of family, friends, and teachers, Anna begins to understand that the similarities between people are more important than the differences, and that people all over the world are connected.

Chapter One
Middle School

$\mathcal{I}$ make my way through the crowded cafeteria to an empty table near the back. There are a few familiar faces, but nobody I really know. I set my tray down, open my lunch bag, and take a bite of my raisin bagel. Last year at North Fairmount Elementary, I always ate lunch with Laura and Camille. After lunch, we went back to Ms. Sylvester's room and she gave us jobs like sharpening pencils or washing the white board. Now Laura is at her new school eating with people I've never met, and Camille is slow to get through the lunch line.

"Hey, Anna, there you are." Camille plops her tray down next to mine. "It takes forever to buy a carton of chocolate milk around here." She pulls her headband down and back up again, then opens the carton and takes a sip. "Do you know which clubs you're going to sign up for?"

I shake my head.

She takes the list out of her backpack. "My mom says I can't join more than three at the very most." Camille has circled the clubs she is interested in. "I can't decide between knitting club, chess club, and C.A.T." She takes a bite of her macaroni and cheese. "What about you?"

The lunchroom is really hot and noisy. A boy is breaking his sandwich into bits and throwing them across the table. I can't imagine staying in this school any longer than I have to. "I don't think I'll join anything for now. Anyway, if I do end up going to China, I'll have to miss a couple of weeks of school."

"You still haven't heard?" Camille raises her eyebrows.

"Ms. Sylvester said they passed the interview. So now they just have to wait."

Camille sighs. "I can't believe it takes this long to adopt a baby."

❋ ❋ ❋

The bell rings and we head to class. The social studies teacher, Ms. Remick, has the schedule on the board. "We will have a shortened period this afternoon," she explains. "To leave time for club shopping."

Our new unit is called "Who Am I?" She asks us to reflect for a minute on what makes us who we are.

Allison raises her hand. "Our parents and grand-parents."

"I was born in China," Camille says. "And that makes me who I am."

I'm always surprised at the way Camille tells every-one she's Chinese. I usually wait, hoping nobody will ask and wishing I could hide my Asian face.

Ms. Remick nods. "Who we are depends on many fac-tors." Ms. Remick continues her explanation. "One of the things that influences each of us is the community we live in. So our first unit will be an oral history project."

Camille pokes me. "What's that?" She always panics when she's not completely sure what's going on, and then she misses the rest of the explanation.

"We will interview people in our communities," Ms. Remick says as she passes out a packet that describes our assignment. "We have to think about whose voices are important to hear and whose voices are often left out." She tells the class to read the instructions and definitions carefully at home and start thinking about a person we might want to interview. The project is due at the end of the semester.

Everybody starts talking at once. Lucy wants to interview her grandpa, and Camille says she might pick Teacher Zhao, from Chinese school. I could interview Ray, the crossing guard, because he likes to talk and he tells good stories. But what does Ms. Remick mean when she says we should consider people whose voices are left out? Is she talking about people we don't know that well? Or people we don't know at all, like Kaylee's birth mother? But it would be impossible to interview someone that you don't know anything about and who you couldn't find no matter how hard you searched.

It's time to pack up and head over to the gym. "Hurry," Camille says, pulling me toward the door.